SUZANNAH ROWNTREE

The Door to Camelot

First published by Bocfodder Press 2019

First edition

Cover art by Wynter Designs

This book was professionally typeset on Reedsy.
Find out more at reedsy.com

Amica mitis, hic liber multos patronos habuit.
Sed, Schuyler, tu maximum fecisti.

Chapter 1

Gloucestershire, AD 1900

Enter these enchanted woods,
You who dare.
Meredith

IT BEGAN ON THE DAY OF her eighteenth birthday. Blanche
Pendragon woke that morning with Simon Corbin's note
burning a hole in her awareness from where it lay under her
pillow. She burrowed a hand under her head to touch the
paper and lay there nibbling her lip in indecision until the
clock downstairs struck half-six in a rich and muffled boom
that echoed through the whole house. As the backwash of
sound faded, Blanche slipped out of bed and began to dress.
Half an hour later she stole out of the house by the back door
and hurried between garden-beds and under blossom-laden
fruit-trees to the gate between the orchard and the hills.

There was a young man leaning against the other side of
the gate, looking out at the hills with folded arms. Blanche
stopped walking. After all, shouldn't she have burned his note
and refused to come? There was still time to slip back to the

1

house, now, before he turned—

He turned and saw her and something that might have been a smile touched his thin secretive lips. All her misgivings faded away and she went up to the gate and put out her hand.

"Good morning, Mr Corbin. I'm sorry if I kept you waiting."

"Good morning, Blanche." Instead of shaking her hand, he bent over it with an oddly ceremonial gesture, and she felt the shiver of his breath across her skin. "Many happy returns of this happy day."

She pulled her hand back, hoping that the sudden pleasurable warmth in her cheeks was not too visible. "You wanted to see me?"

"Yes." He indicated a bag in the grass at his feet. "I am on my way to Lydney to catch the London train, and I could not allow your birthday to pass without some token of my regard."

There. See? It was all perfectly proper and respectable. Blanche felt a little contemptuous of herself for the scruples that had haunted her since Kitty Walker passed his note to her yesterday afternoon.

Mr Corbin reached into the pocket of his coat and drew out a box, which he presented with a flourish. "Miss Pendragon."

She slipped off the lid and took out a little hourglass hanging on a silver pivot from a black ribbon, its belly full of twinkling black sand.

"Oh, it's beautiful!"

"You like it."

Her guardian, the antiquarian, who invested every colour, gemstone, beast, and planet with arcane and symbolic meaning, would likely give her a lecture on saturnine influences. Blanche decided not to care. "Yes, I do." She threw a wry smile up at Mr Corbin. "Sir Ector wouldn't."

He reached out and closed her hand over the box. "Then don't wear it where he will see it."

She couldn't do that; if her guardian didn't see the pendant, her lady's-companion Nerys would, and both of them would be hurt by her attempted deceit. Blanche smiled, trying to look daring and devil-may-care. "Oh, I'm not afraid to wear it. And thank you. It was sweet of you to walk so far out of your way." She backed a few steps, signalling that it was time for him to move on and catch his train.

"Wait," he said, and leaned over the gate. "Miss Walker means to take a motor to Tintern Abbey next week. Won't you come?"

"Oh! I'd love to. When will it be?"

"Sunday."

Blanche's face fell. "Oh. *Perhaps* Sir Ector would let me go. But there will be church, and…"

The beginnings of a smile pulled at Mr Corbin's face. "Oh, the Galilean can spare you for a day, surely?"

She bit her lip to keep from smiling, and failed. He saw, and the amusement deepened in the corners of his mouth.

"Yet one day I shall convince you to become a Freethinker, too."

"Oh, I could never do that." But she did admire the casual way he carried it off, as if impiety was no great risk to a man of his worth. She backed another step. "Maybe Sir Ector will let me come. I'll ask. No, I'll beg." And with a laugh, she hurried away as quickly as she had come.

AT DINNER THAT EVENING, SIR ECTOR L'Espée was talking about the relief of Kimberly when he inevitably lost himself in historical minutiae and began lecturing on Roman cavalry. At last he paused between caltrops and stirrups to sip his wine and Nerys, from the other side of the table, said: "Blanche dear, I've never seen that before."

Blanche put her fingers up to the hourglass around her neck, and her heart sank a little. So there *would* be trouble. "It was a gift."

Sir Ector put down his wineglass, dabbed at his frost-white moustache, and leaned closer to see. "Someone has a morbid taste. Who was it?"

"It's from Simon Corbin."

"When did he call?" Nerys did not change her expression, or the mild tone of her voice, but Blanche thought she could sense reproof.

"I was walking this morning and met him going down to the train at Lydney. It wasn't improper in the *least*."

Nerys's eyebrow flickered up at Blanche's defensive tone, but she made no further comment. Only the air around her grew a little cooler. Blanche sensed that, too, and heaved a sigh at her plate, wishing Nerys could forget about being a chaperone, just for a moment.

Sir Ector said, "Have him come to dinner some day. I should like to meet your friend Simon Corbin."

Blanche poked at her food. "All right. I'll tell him next time."

Sir Ector looked at Nerys. Nerys looked at Blanche. "You know that your guardian would prefer to know your friends, Blanche. Especially such a close friend as Mr Corbin."

"I know it," said Blanche. She kept her voice sweet, but spoiled the effect by stabbing a potato. "He isn't such a close friend, anyway. I'll give the hourglass back if you don't like it."

Sir Ector blinked and said, "Give it back? Not if you really like it, Blanche."

She nodded and took another bite, not looking away from

her food. After a moment's silence, Sir Ector's fork scraped his plate and she knew the discussion was over. But silence hung on them all, becoming more difficult to lift with every moment. Blanche felt a quiver of melancholy in the air and glanced opposite, to Nerys.

It was odd that her young companion, who went so quietly clad in grey with never one black hair out of place, who spoke so reluctantly and so rarely changed expression, should be so legible in her moods. It was also odd that nothing seemed bleaker than Nerys's melancholy, which might only be provoked by a birthday dinner gone sour, but held in itself all the tears shed since the beginning of the world. Blanche felt sorry for her petulance over the hourglass. She gathered all of her strength against the chill in the air and said with cumbersome gaiety:

"Why, Nerys, you look so thoughtful. Come, stop frowning like that. The wind will change, and where will you be then?" She leaned forward and whispered. "Remember what happened to the Queen when Prince Albert died—they say the wind changed at the funeral and she *never smiled again.*"

Nerys looked up gravely. "I'd not heard it." But there was a silver shimmer through the tone of her voice that hinted at laughter deep below the surface, and her shoulders went back a little, and the mood in the room lightened.

Blanche turned to Sir Ector. "Kitty Walker has asked me to go with some friends to see Tintern Abbey on Sunday, in the new motor-car."

"Sunday?" Sir Ector frowned.

"I know," Blanche said, "but Kitty's London friends are visiting, and I've never been riding in a motor before. And I haven't missed a service once this year."

"You might miss Evensong on Sunday, then. Perhaps Miss Walker can delay her excursion until after the morning service."

"I'll ask her." It was, she supposed, the most she could hope for. Still, it would be too bad to miss the jaunt and spoil the day for the sake of a few hours at church.

They finished dinner and went into the library, where Blanche made tea for Nerys and herself and coffee for Sir Ector. Nerys took a book into a corner, but Blanche stood in front of the fire to warm herself, leaving her saucer on the tray so that she could curl both hands around the teacup. Sir Ector sank into an armchair.

"Well!" he said in a comfortable murmur.

She turned and smiled, unsure whether he was about to make a birthday speech or relapse into another comfortable silence.

"Well," he repeated, "you're eighteen, Blanche."

The birthday speech it would be. "Yes. Not for another forty-two years will the word 'sweet' alliterate with my age."

He smiled as though he hadn't heard the joke, and she realised that a birthday speech was no time for banter. He'd laced his fingers together and was running each thumb in turn over the other.

"Blanche, I…there's something I've been putting off telling you. About your parents."

Her parents.

She'd never known them. She didn't even know their names. It was years now since she'd been curious.

Why had he waited until now?

Something hot fell onto her hand and Blanche looked down to see the tea in her cup rippling. She took a deep breath, replaced the cup on its saucer, and wiped her fingers before asking, "Is it very bad? The truth, I mean?"

"No, no." Sir Ector's voice died away. At last he looked at her under bushy brows, almost shyly, as if in fear of some rejection. "You may find it difficult to believe."

A quick, warm affection rose in her throat for him. "Tell me and see."

Sir Ector looked into the fire, fidgeting with something in his pocket.

"I have something for you," he said at last. "It was your mother's." And he drew out the thing in his pocket and held it up to her.

The ring Blanche took from him was antique silver, cabochon-set with a glimmering moonstone. Her mother's ring! Blanche folded it into her hand and held tightly to the only thing her parents had left her. There had never been anything else, not even a faded photograph or some old letters.

"I don't even know her name."

"Look inside."

There was a lamp on the mantelpiece and Blanche held the ring up to its pearly glow. Spidery engraved letters ran all round the inside of the band. " 'Guinevera casta vera.' Guinevera?"

"Your mother."

Blanche twisted the ring onto her finger, thinking what a sentimental old-fashioned couple they must have been, rather like her guardian with his old gallantries and his Old French. She couldn't resist a chuckle. "What was my father's name? 'Arthur, King of the Britons'?"

Before the words crossed her lips, Blanche knew they were a mistake. Sir Ector dropped his head, and the shadows hid his face. When he rose, that shyly eager air was gone and he thrust his hands into his pockets with feigned briskness. "Well," he said, "that reminds me. I must work on my address to the

7

Newport Antiquities Society."

Over in the corner, Nerys rustled to her feet.

"No, forgive me," Blanche begged, feeling inarticulately guilty, as if she had killed something small and helpless by accident. "I shouldn't have joked like that. Won't you tell me some more about them?"

Sir Ector smiled wistfully and kissed her forehead. "Soon, Blanche. When you're ready to hear. Goodnight."

"Goodnight." She went to the door and held it open for Nerys, who had the tea-tray. The lady's-companion passed and went down the hall, but Blanche lingered, looking back from the threshold. "Still—my father. Can't you tell me his name? Please? Now that I know Mother's?"

Sir Ector, riffling through the papers on his desk, stopped at the sound of her voice and leaned his hands on the oil-smooth wood. He didn't look up; only his shoulders lifted, then sank in a long slow sigh.

"No," he said, and to Blanche's ears, there was a bald honesty in his voice that allowed only one interpretation.

"Well, goodnight." Blanche, trying not to let mortification seep into her voice, closed the door, and went slowly down the dark corridor to the stairs. In her unlit room she looked again at the ring clenched in her hand, but now it was only a glint in the starlight. So it *was* very bad. A sense of revulsion gripped her stomach, contempt both for herself and for her mother. *Casta vera!*

She tossed the ring onto her dressing-table and began to undress. She was sitting at the table in her nightgown and peignoir, unpinning her hair, when a knock came on the door and Nerys entered.

Blanche glanced up and forced a smile. Nerys, without a

word, picked up the hairbrush and began to work on Blanche's hair. It was no part of her duties, but Nerys was as patient with knots as with everything else, and Blanche leaned back with a little sigh. She stared at the two heads in the mirror, her own flame-haired, day-eyed; Nerys's moon-skinned, night-haired. After a moment she put her hands up to her throat and took off the little black hourglass.

She wondered why, since they so obviously distrusted Simon Corbin, Sir Ector and Nerys couldn't state their suspicions plainly. Was it because he was a Freethinker? At least, she thought with a twinge, a Freethinker would think no less of her for being ill-born.

She put the hourglass on the table next to the moonstone ring and said, "I like Mr Corbin, and I hoped you would like him too."

Nerys looked through the mirror at her with a glimmer of surprise, but then dropped her eyes back to Blanche's tawny-red hair.

Blanche spoke as patiently as she knew how. "What's the matter? Why do you not approve of him?"

Nerys shook her head. "I hardly know him well enough to approve or disapprove. I've only spoken to him once."

"I know he isn't conventional," Blanche said. "But he always speaks his mind and he doesn't let other people shame him into thinking differently."

"I think…" said Nerys.

She so rarely put the shifting transparency of her moods into words. "Go on," said Blanche, when the silence threatened to lengthen.

"I think it will take you a long time to know such a man. I cannot read him at all." She lifted worried eyes to Blanche.

"He is so full of news and events," Blanche said. "I like to hear about such things without getting tangled up in Roman cavalry tactics."

Nerys smiled before she could stop herself, and then tried to look disapproving. Blanche laughed at her. Nerys moved further up Blanche's hair, changing the subject.

"Are you going on errands with Emmeline tomorrow?"

"I did all my visiting today."

"Really? You went to see Mrs Jones, and the bricklayer's family?"

"No." Blanche picked up her mother's ring and fidgeted. "We met Kitty when we stopped in the street, and then we ran out of time to chatter Welsh with the parishioners."

It was, of course, unfair to say *we*, because it was no one's fault but hers that the time had run away, and no vicar's daughter could be more conscientious than Emmeline.

"Oh, Blanche. You know what Sir Ector says."

"I know." Blanche quoted. " 'A wise princess will not only feel sorrow when she sees people in affliction, but roll up her sleeves and help them as much as she can.' It's from that medieval book he gave me for my last birthday. I had to translate the whole thing from Middle French."

"You will be grateful for it one day," said Nerys, in a gentle tone that robbed the words of any possible sting.

Blanche grimaced. "I sometimes think that Sir Ector sees himself as some medieval lord, and me as a medieval princess. What will he ask me to do next? Intercede with him for the peasantry, as Christine de Pisan recommends, or learn siege warfare so that I can defend the house while he's away?"

"Both a good use of your time," said Nerys, with no hint of laughter. "When do you mean to visit Mrs Jones?"

"Christine said to send alms by a servant, and anonymously, 'by the example of monseigneur Saint Nicholas'." She shot an impudent grin at Nerys, and then admitted, "Emmeline will be busy tomorrow with the Infants' Bible Study. We have agreed to go the day after, so you need not worry. In the meantime I shall be as medieval as I know how, and languish about like Burne-Jones's Briar Rose."

THAT NIGHT SHE DREAMED ABOUT THE King again.

She stood in a riverside meadow between greenwood and castle. Overhead the sun shone gilt in a sky like powdered lapis and struck golden sparks from the King's blood-red dragon banner.

For the hundredth time, she half-closed her eyes against the fiery colour of meadow flowers and silken pavilions. For the hundredth time a blinding glint from someone's mailed shoulder forced her to blink and turn her head to see the King.

In crown and heraldic red robes, bearded, belted, bear-like, he sat enthroned by an oak tree with two wolf-hounds at his feet. Youthful vigour lay couchant in his gigantic limbs and in his big veined hands, but his level look was grave and wise. There was a sheathed sword lying across his knees, and his fingers moved up and down the scabbard as though it could make music.

A harper sat at his right hand, mouth open in song. At something the minstrel said, graceful feminine heads swayed and laughed all around, and white hands clapped, scattering flashes of colour from undersleeve and lining. Yet no sound reached Blanche's ears. Unlike the vision, it had been lost long ago.

By the King on his left hand sat the Queen in a shower of

silver-blonde hair that fell unbound to her hips. When she smiled it was to herself, secretly, as if to a jest only she heard. With the ladies round about she was tying may-thorn hoops, but then she looked up—this was Blanche's favourite part—and her mouth seemed to shape Blanche's name. In a turmoil of green robes she came forward, arms opening.

BLANCHE WOKE.

On most nights it was easy to turn over and go back to sleep, but tonight wakefulness caught and held. At last she slid out of bed and tiptoed to her dressing-table, feeling across it for her mother's ring. It slid onto her finger. She couldn't feel the spidery words against her skin, but she remembered them. *Guinevere.*

Guinevere was the name of a queen from legend. Like the one in the dream she had had since childhood.

Impossible thoughts wheeled through her mind.

In the next room, she heard Nerys moving, opening her wardrobe door...

For years, Nerys had woken her at midnight on her birthday, and they had stolen downstairs to have hot cocoa and cake by the kitchen fire. Blanche was much too old for midnight feasts now, of course. And it was a night too late. Still...they were both awake. And she wanted some company.

Blanche shrugged into her peignoir and went out into the hall. There was no answer to her tap at Nerys's door. Blanche hesitated, and nearly gave up and went back to bed. Then she remembered the creak of the wardrobe door. Perhaps she had knocked too softly. She twisted the handle, cracked the door ajar, and peeped in, whispering, "Nerys?"

There was light in the room. The curtains had been pulled

back, and moonlight pooled on the floor. But the wardrobe door also sat ajar, and from it came a warm golden glow...

Nerys was nowhere to be seen.

Blanche assumed, yawning, that Nerys must have left a lamp burning in there. It seemed a dangerous thing to do, and she closed the door behind her and crossed the room to the wardrobe.

She opened the door and saw at once that there was no lamp. It was more like...

...more like *daylight*.

Blanche blinked at the light, and her heart skipped a little faster, but she was too curious to be frightened. Instead she ducked her head and stepped through the wardrobe door.

SHE EMERGED FROM A BIG WOODEN chest, up-ended so that its lid functioned like a door. Blanche glanced about her, and for a moment imagined that her childhood dream had come to life. A swift rush of gladness took her by the throat and almost knocked her to her knees. It was just like waking the morning after a nightmare to discover that one's worst fears had not, after all, come true. Then she shook herself, a little ashamed of the notion. Did she *want* to live in a picture-book? And her waking life was hardly a nightmare. She looked around again, with a more critical eye.

She stood in a pavilion, surrounded by the spicy smell of the woods on a warm spring morning full of light and birdsong. The pavilion itself was just like the ones in her dream, made of imperious saffron-coloured silk that rippled in the morning breeze. Sunlight filtered through the wall and drenched the pavilion's interior with rosy light.

It was like standing inside a jewel, and the pavilion's furniture was rich enough to do it justice. There was a couch, chairs, and a low table all made from carved and inlaid wood. On the table goblets and bread and apples and roasted meat were set out.

And still Nerys was nowhere to be seen.

Blanche stood without moving for a space, head bent to listen. Apart from the sighing of the breeze and the sound of birds, she could hear nothing. She was in a lonely place, then, and not (alas!) in the busy meadow of her dream.

Curious to see the place to which she had wandered, she began to move forward, lifting her eyes from the ground—and with a gasp, saw she was no longer alone. The flap of the tent was still falling without a whisper of sound behind a newcomer.

He was young and savage and dirty, reeking of horses, clad in skins. There was a knife almost as long as her forearm strapped to his calf, and he carried a pair of javelins with knapped-stone blades point-down in one hand.

He spoke.

"Duw a rodo da ywch, arglwyddes."

Chapter 2

Logres

—O mother
How can ye keep me tether'd to you?—Shame.
Man am I grown, a man's work must I do.
Follow the deer? Follow Christ, the King,
Live pure, speak true, right wrong, follow the King—
Else, wherefore born?
Tennyson

IN THE DAYS WHEN A MAN might travel from one end of
Britain to the other without leaving the shade of the greenwood
if he kept his word, let his sword rest lightly in its sheath, and
watched for foes, when roads were hard to find and friends
harder, and fire and steel the first necessities of life—long ago,
deep in the hills of Wales, there lived a boy and his mother.

The boy's name was Perceval, and all the days he could
remember he had run wild in the woods wearing deerskin and
wolfpelts, knowing no enemies but wolves and wolf's-head
outlaws, knowing no human company but that of his mother.
But hers was enough. In her stories, in the long passages she
had him memorise, and in the unknown languages in which

she drilled him until he could speak and understand them with ease, lay a door to the outside world that had captured his imagination.

This could be ignored in the winter, when the world was dead and the cold and hunger bit so hard that survival took all their time and energy. But when each spring came and the sun gathered warmth and the whole forest woke into life, the call sounded more insistently to leave the hidden hills and go out into the world of men and deeds.

Last spring, for the first time, he had told his mother what he felt, for the need to be up and doing was too strong now to be ignored.

"I know I must stay and care for you, Mother," he finished, half ashamed of the confession.

But she sat silently for a while and her answer, when it came, was the last thing he expected.

"Oh, Perceval, a falcon is born to hunt, and so are you. One day you will hunt indeed—but not yet."

"Why? Am I not ready?"

She looked at him sadly and said, "Give me a little longer."

That year his mother had barely given him a moment's rest. Odd requests sent him roaming far into the wilds or kept him scratching figures into the walls of their cave: the kindling of a lantern on a rocky western coast, a calculation of how the stars would stand at the vernal equinox. Old lessons, too, had to be repeated from beginning to end, and discussed in conversations that tested not only his grasp of the contents but also his fluency in the Latin, or Greek, or occasionally even Saxon or Irish to which his mother would change mid-speech.

This spring the call was back, biting harder than ever.

He had prowled far to the north on this particular morning,

armed with the slender darts he made himself, when he saw the riders.

There were three of them, mailed and jingling. At their saddlebows hung vivid shields and iron helms; by their stirrups rode lances. In the dappled wood they made a bright splash of colour, and Perceval was pierced with the longing to ride with them to strange countries and stranger adventures.

On that impulse he stepped out into the road and hailed them.

The strangers reined in. Startled hands tightened on hilts and lances, but then relaxed at the sight of the boy in wolf-pelts. "Who calls?" asked the foremost, a dark man with a lean scarred face.

"First tell me who *you* are," said Perceval, so eager that his breath lagged behind his words. "Do you come from Heaven like the angels? Or are you fays from the other world?"

"Neither," was the answer. "We are not angels, though we serve the King of Heaven. Of the elves you, perhaps, may know more than we do."

"What are you, then?"

"Men. Knights who serve Arthur Pendragon the High King. I, Lancelot, hold these lands of him."

Perceval stood stock-still, thinking, for so long that the man went on with a smile: "Will you hold for me a corner of this wood? Then you may catechise whom you wish."

"No; only tell me this," said Perceval. "Where may I find your King? I should like to be a knight."

One of the men behind Lancelot coughed as though smothering a laugh, but Lancelot replied gravely. "I counsel you to go in search of him, sir, for it is the Pendragon's chief delight to grant such boons to bold men. Yet there are conditions. You

17

must keep yourself either to gentle words or hard blows, and you must defend the weak and poor."

"I will do these things," said Perceval with a gesture of easy assurance, and the knight smiled again.

"Then travel east and a little south. When you come to broader lands there will be others to point the way."

Perceval lifted his darts in salute. "We will meet again," he said, and vanished into the forest.

THAT EVENING WHEN PERCEVAL CAME HOME his mother was sitting outside the cave, sewing in the last light of the sun. He exchanged greetings and dropped to a crouch beside her. Words had never come to him with difficulty, and he had had all afternoon to think the matter over.

"I went north today," he told her without preface, "and I met three knights who said they served the High King Arthur and the King of Heaven. And there is nothing else in the world I would rather do or be."

As she had the year before when he first told her his dreams, his mother sat in silence. Her needle went in and out of the patch on her old blue cloak many times before she answered, and the sadness was there in her voice again, but heavier. "Perceval, you must understand. It is not an easy life: full of wanderings, woundings, dangers, and death. In the end, always death."

"But those come to us and all mortals, Mother. Why! Would you discourage me, after all this time?"

For the length of a breath, her face was still and pale as stone. "To all mortals, yes. I know this is your calling, Perceval. But I cannot follow you when you go. If you go east, I must go west, and an end will come of me in Britain. Will you not stay

18

another year?"

"No, Mother." He pointed to the chain about her neck. "I must follow my father's calling. You said it yourself on the night of the frost, when I speared the man from the hills."

"Then you have guessed," she said. "Yes. It was the Pendragon of Britain whom your father served, and loved better than a brother. And your father gave this to me before you were born." She lifted the chain over her head. From it hung a golden ring with a fire-red stone.

"Tell me why," he said, as he had when he was a little boy.

Her lips moved in a weary smile. "A knight will give a lady a ring from his hand and take a kiss from her lips, when he wishes to love her and serve her all his days," she recited, as she had when he was small. She pulled the ring from the chain and held it out to him. "This ring is the knight's who swore to serve me. Take it. One day you may find a lady to wear it."

Before the sun was up, Perceval kissed his mother goodbye. "Go to the King at Camelot," she told him. "Remember what I have taught you. Your father was among the mightiest of the knights of Logres."

"I will be a son worthy of him."

Perceval's mother looked up at him. Her grey eyes opened on him like fathomless wells of thought. Perceval found himself holding his breath dizzily to hear the echo of his words splashing into their depths.

"And you will be a son worthy of him," she said. Then he blinked, and she was his mother again; and she turned her head aside so that he could see only the white swell of her cheek, but heard her sigh: "Alas…"

He rode away in the rain on Llech, his little grey pony. His mother stood outside the cave watching him go; she waved once when he looked back. Then Perceval fixed his eyes on the forest ahead, and knew that the trees were clouding her from view, and he never saw her in the world again but once.

HE WOUND DOWN THROUGH THE WOODS and hills of Wales, sometimes walking and sometimes riding the clammy, muddy little pony he had taken for the journey. The rain drizzled steadily, dripped down his neck, and turned the pony's grey coat black. In the soggy valleys, Llech's hooves sank deep into the mire. It occurred to Perceval once that perhaps summer would be a pleasanter time for travel. But it never came into his mind to look back now, with the world and adventure ahead.

When he came to the River Usk, at the border of his world, he forded it, turned, and followed it south-east through the hills, pressing on as quickly as possible, up strange hill and down unknown dale until the land around him began to change. The hills fell gentler and lower, the trees thinned, and the river gathered strength and girth.

It was late on the second day, as the sun began to set, that he emerged from the forest and stared down one last long slope to a rolling plain, where the Usk turned and ran away south to the sea. Perceval stared at the scene in amazement. All his life he had lived in thickly-wooded hill-country. There were more hills and trees in the distance, but down in the plain lay short-cropped pastures with many sheep and cattle, the first farmland he had seen.

He rode down the hill, turning his head from side to side to drink in the view. Far away on the right, he glimpsed the sea and what might be more land beyond.

Perceval rode straight to the village, but was stopped by the sentry at the gate, who came running out of the little guard-house pulling on his helm. He squinted at Perceval and snapped, "What do you want here?"

"Your hospitality, fair sir," said Perceval. "I have travelled far today."

"Go on!" said the gate-warden. "You're one of those elvish folk from the hills. Steal a man's breath from his mouth if it weren't nailed down."

Perceval blinked in surprise. "I—"

"No," said the gate-warden. "Move on. We've trouble enough without your kind adding to it." He put his hands on his hips and planted himself in the gate, glowering.

"Certainly. Only tell me in which direction is Camelot."

"Straight east. Why are you riding there?"

"To be a knight," replied the wild boy, and faded into the dusk with his dirty pony before the man could gather breath to reply. Before night he had coaxed Llech to swim the river and was among the trees on the other side.

Perceval lit a fire, huddled into his pelts, and closed his eyes. He was hardened to the cold and wet and slept lightly, darts in hand. Long before dawn came, he toasted the last of his mother's bread over the reawakened fire and was on his way across the hills, straight for the rising sun. He camped near the Wye that evening, found a ford by which to cross in the morning, and kept on until he came to a high treeless ridge overlooking low wooded hills and the glimmer of water, and saw nestled within them green pastures studded with little farms and animals like ants. The distant lowlands looked sunny and warm, but up here on the ridge blew an icy wind that seemed to turn the sun cold.

There was one tree, an oak, not very old, but gnarled and

disfigured. On it a brace of ravens sat complaining. If there had been a stone lying on the ground, Perceval would have tossed it at them.

He was distracted from his surroundings by Llech, who buried his head in the grass and began tearing up wads of it, roots and all. Perceval slid down from the pony's back, letting the halter trail on the ground. Llech moved off a pace or two. "Well, then," Perceval said to him. "Eat if you like, but I see a pool down the hill, and I am thirsty enough to swallow all of it."

He strode through the grass, then slid down the steep slope, taking care not to make a sound, for he was beginning to hunger for fresh meat. At the slope's foot he found a little, dark, deep mere, with strands of early-morning fog still clinging to its surface, very secret in the hills and the wood. But Perceval saw immediately that he was not alone. There on the other side of the lake, mirrored in its surface, stood a bright saffron-coloured pavilion still limp with morning dew.

Perceval went warily toward the strange structure. Trampled grass showed where horses and men had walked around the pavilion, but he could hear no sound of voice or harness. He lifted the tent flap and went in.

There was a gasp, and he was looking into the startled face of a tall and stately damsel, crowned with hair like flame.

BLANCHE WAS SURE, NOW, THAT SHE wasn't dreaming. Her heart was hammering too hard for this to be a dream.

The young savage spoke again in the shushing tone she used herself to calm a horse. *"Duw a rodo da ywch"*—but now suddenly the words made sense to her. It was Welsh. It was a greeting in Welsh. She knew Welsh because Sir Ector insisted that she practice it often when she went to visit poor folk in the village.

"Good morning," she said in the same language, and swallowed hard.

He looked at the food on the table by the couch. "I have travelled far, damsel, and am very hungry."

Blanche edged away from the table, closer to the wooden chest which led back into Nerys's bedroom. "Eat," she said with an imploring gesture.

He went to the table, dropped into a low crouch, and began to eat with great tearing bites, never taking his eyes from her face. Caught in that gaze she dared not turn and bolt into the wooden chest, so she stood motionless staring back at him. He was lean and brown, all bone and sinew. There were white scars and scabbed cuts on his bare arms and legs and the skin wrinkled like old leather at his knees and elbows. Above all that his face was incongruously young, so young that she began to fear him a little less. Then for the first time she really saw the look in his eyes, so frankly admiring that she turned her head away with an angry blush, and the taste of dread came back.

He ate half of the food exactly: one of the bannocks, one of the apples, and one of the collops of meat, wolfed down in less time than she thought possible. There were two cups on the table as well, and when he had finished everything else, he sniffed and tasted the wine. Immediately he spat it onto the grass.

"It has gone sour," he said, seeing her horrified look.

She shook her head at him, lest he suspect her of meaning him harm. "It's wine. It should taste like that."

He replaced the goblet on the table and rose to his feet,

picking up the javelins again.

"I thank you for the food, damsel," he said, but he made no move to leave. Blanche tried to think of something to say, but before she could open her mouth he moved forward and caught her hand, even as she shied away. She smelled smoke and sweat and horse.

"Be not frightened," he said, very earnestly, pulling her back to face him. "I will serve you. I will give you a ring for this one."

She looked at him blankly, then glanced down at her hand.

The ring of Guinevere.

"It was my mother's," she murmured, but her mouth had gone dry and no sound came from her lips, and she was already reaching up with her free hand to pull off the jewel. Let him have it, if he would only leave her. And who was her mother, anyway?

He took the ring and dropped it into the pouch that hung from his belt, and produced another, gold with a blood-red stone, which he slid onto her hand where her mother's ring had been.

"I thank you, damsel." And he leaned forward and kissed her, very quickly but fiercely, on the mouth.

When he had kissed her he released her and fell back a step, looking doubtful, as if suddenly aware that he had trespassed some boundary. At that look Blanche's mind began to work again, and she found she was clenching her hands into fists by her sides.

"You had best run," she told him coldly. "My guardian is near, and if he finds you here he will kill you."

He fell back another few steps, said "Be well, damsel," and turning on his heel left as silently as he had come. Only the flap of the pavilion shivered to show that he had been.

Blanche stood rigid for as long as it took to count to a hundred before she sank onto the couch. Now that the boy had left, she began to shake. In vain she told herself that he had not hurt her, and (after another moment) that she did not think he would have. She threw her arms around herself in an absurdly literal attempt to pull herself together. And what of the country in the wardrobe? And what of the sun, shining in the night?

There was a rustling sound in the grass outside, and Blanche bolted to her feet. If it should be the boy again—

It was Nerys: hair loose, robed in blue, looking more like a queen than a lady's companion. But when she saw how Blanche was trembling, she came forward with quick compassion.

Blanche flew into her arms and gasped, "Oh, Nerys—I was looking for you, and there was a savage man, and—"

"Shh," Nerys said, as if she were a mother comforting a frightened child. "Nimue never—I didn't know of it until a moment ago."

Blanche pulled away when she realised that she had been clinging for safety to a woman whose head nearly fitted under her chin. In embarrassment she changed the subject. "Nerys, why is it morning here?"

Nerys sighed, a long slow breath of regret. Instead of answering, she said, "Blanche, you're very tired. Sleep."

"No," Blanche protested. She wrenched away from Nerys and staggered toward the pavilion door with some idea of retrieving her mother's ring, if she could. "He won't be far—"

The words thickened like syrup on her tongue, even as she pulled aside the flap of the pavilion. Outside, she saw a dark pool and a forest under a bleak ridge. She took another step forward, missed her footing, and fell…

WHEN BLANCHE OPENED HER EYES, SHE was curled into her own warm bed early on a frosty spring morning.

So it had all been a dream. She could even feel the cabochon-set ring on her finger; the threads of worry, pulled tight in her mind, came loose and drifted. She had woken from the nightmare, and it was not true after all.

She slid the ring off her finger and brought it out from under the covers. But it was not her mother's ring. Red-gold it shone in the grey dawn light, red-gold as the ring which the stranger in the pavilion had given her.

Chapter 3

For if he live, that hath you done despite,
He shall you do due recompense again,
Or else his wrong with greater puissance maintain.
Spenser

IT WAS A FEAST-DAY WHEN PERCEVAL came to the High King's city of Camelot, riding in an uneasy fog of thought, for he began to wonder if his mother might not have meant something different by her instructions about the ring. Once he had become a knight, he thought, he would go in quest of the damsel of the pavilion, and if he had done wrong, he might yet give her reason to forgive him.

Camelot castle stood on a hill in a low wide valley opening toward a plain on the south, a labyrinthine many-spired place melting into the noisy little town at its feet. A river came down out of the northern hills to moat the town and castle, the eastern bank of which was good black farmland, but the western bank was weaving forest.

Llech distrusted the bridge. He stepped onto it only after persuasion, and when he heard the hollow thud of his hooves on the wood he threw up his head and plunged into the crowded street, swerving around to face the echoes when he had reached safety. Perceval, accustomed to riding bareback, kept his seat easily and glanced about for the sentries. They stared, but made no move to challenge him. And no wonder! Turning Llech to continue up the street, Perceval saw farmers, beggars, knights, tumblers, jugglers, minstrels, kegs of ale, and the blazing colours of best clothes.

Someone called out, "Come and have a drink, stranger!" but Perceval replied, "Not I! I am going to the King."

His voice was almost swallowed by a ringing clatter on the bridge. Llech shied around again to see, and Perceval saw a knight in gilded armour upon a mighty horse like a thunderhead bearing down upon them. For a confused moment Perceval's pony planted his feet and balked. A voice grated out of the knight's helm, "Way, fellow," and the iron figure hefted the butt of his spear to sweep Perceval aside. In the nick of time Llech danced out of the way. With a rush the knight clattered past, up the hill toward the keep, leaving merrymakers tossed in his wake.

"Follow that oafish one," someone called to Perceval. "He's off to the King, no doubt."

Perceval heard and dug his heels into the pony's sides. Up the hill they cantered among the protests left in the knight's trail, and trotted beneath a massive carved door-lintel into a high-roofed hall rippling with bright banners. Here under soaring arches in the light of a hundred high windows stood a great round table in the midst of the hall, scores of men seated around it talking and eating and laughing. Perceval looked once, then again, and his stomach quaked as he realised that he was in the presence of the greatest warriors of the world, each one tried and tempered on the field of war.

Could he prove himself worthy to sit among them? For the

space of a breath he was glad that none of them saw him come in. They were falling silent, staring at the gilded knight, who trotted between the round table and the long straight tables that flanked it on each side toward the King's seat at the head of the hall.

Here at the Table the King sat enthroned (pewter-grey hair the King had, and the marks of war on his hands, but piercing eyes that would be wise in judgement); the pale Queen stood beside him with an upraised goblet of silver and glass, and words dying away on her lips. The gilded knight swung down from his horse and strode toward them without a pause. "Who is this," he shouted, "who is this that stands at the head of the Round Table to pledge them all to truth and virtue, and is herself no better than a common stale?"

There was the rattle of a chair sliding across cobbles, a raking up of rushes, and a flash of light as a blade was drawn. One of the knights, on the far side of the table, was on his feet, moving—the King, more slowly, rose from his seat—the gilded knight snatched the cup from the Queen's hand even while he spoke.

And flung the wine in her face.

"A fig for the Table," the ruffian was shouting, with a laugh, over the uproar of shouts and falling chairs. Perceval saw the King say a soft word, and a lean grey shadow leaped from under his chair. The gilded knight vaulted to his horse as the hound sprang with bared teeth and straining red maw for his heels. Then the warhorse neighed and lashed out with a hoof. The dog scrabbled uselessly across the floor; another heartbeat, and the gilded knight was gone with the drumming of hooves.

Above it all the Queen of Britain stood still, wine dripping from her face, her mouth pressed shut in a white and wordless fury which swept impersonally across Perceval and all the people gathered in the hall before alighting on the King. Arthur turned to meet it and with a curiously practical gesture offered her a napkin. Then everyone was talking at once—the knights around the table, the ladies in the galleries above, the plain people at their low tables. But in the midst of the commotion, the man who had risen from his seat at the table when the strange knight first snatched the Queen's cup now sheathed his sword, stalked up the hall to the King and said, low and grinding: "Give me leave, lord, and I'll beat him like a dog."

It was the hawk-faced knight Perceval had met in the Welsh forest, the man called Lancelot. His words would have gone unmarked in the clamour but for the hush which fell upon the hall when he came to the King.

Every face was turned upon the knight Lancelot as he stood before the High King of Britain. The Queen bent her head and pressed the napkin to her eyes. Only the injured hound whimpered from the corner.

Crash! A knotted fist smacked the table, making the cups jump, and its owner—a stocky, bull-headed man—growled, "Sire! I'll go."

"Gawain!" said Lancelot. "Of your courtesy, this is my fight. Sire, give me the quest!"

Perceval knew that if he waited another moment his own chance would pass. He kicked Llech into a trot and rode to the head of the table, scattering attendants. "My lord king, a boon!"

The King had stood unmoved amid the outcry, but when Perceval spoke he turned his head and looked from the muddy pony to its skin-clad rider, and a gleam shone in his eye. "Speak, good fellow."

30

"My lord, send me to avenge this insult, and let me receive knighthood when I have proven myself."

"What!" A very tall man who, when the knight came, had leaned back and begun to crack nuts, laughed at Perceval. "Look at him! Darts and rabbit-skin armour! One look down that knight's spear and he'll run back to his pig-pen. Go away, boy, this is work for knights."

If Perceval had doubts about facing the enemy knight, he lost them now. "I came here to be knighted," he said loud enough for everyone to hear, "but I see I must have an iron pot to put my head in. Very good! I will ride after that knight and equip me with his spoils, and I will bring back the goblet to the Queen."

The man laughed again. But one of the damsels who had come to tend the Queen went to Perceval smiling.

"Sir Perceval, the flower of knighthood," she said. And she curtseyed to him.

The tall man jumped up, knocking his chair over behind him. "Spiteful imp! You live here a year, refusing to smile or speak, and now you smile at this puppy in the face of King Arthur and the Table Round, and call him the flower of knighthood?" Before Perceval could stop him, he had reached out and cuffed the girl's ear.

"Kay," said the King, quietly, but Perceval saw the man named Kay flinch at his tone like a dog coming to heel. "Will you prove the knights of the Table no better than their enemies? Be sure you will suffer for that." He turned to Perceval. "I grant your boon, boy. Follow that stranger. When you return bearing the cup, and wearing the armour, the knighthood is yours."

Perceval did not hear the murmur of protest that rose in the hall; he hissed in a breath through teeth clenched on the foretaste of victory. He had no words for thanks, but he bowed his head low to the mane of his pony. Before he turned, he spoke to the knight called Kay. "I also swear—when I return, you will pay for that blow." He set heels to Llech's sides and went out the gate and down the hill at a reckless canter.

Folk at the castle gate pointed north when he asked in a shout for directions, and Perceval and his pony went thundering up the road, the mount toiling gamely, the rider laughing and brandishing his darts.

PERCEVAL CAUGHT UP WITH THE THIEF of the goblet a league from Camelot on a slope running down into the forest. The knight was walking his horse, evidently not in dread of pursuit, and though he glanced behind when he first heard Llech's hooves, he paid no more attention to the pony or its rider until Perceval came within a spear's length and hallooed. "Turn around and face me, coward knight!"

Ahead, the knight yanked his horse around and gripped his lance. "Do you think to fight me?" he asked, laughter in his voice. "Which swine-shed did they raid to find you?"

"They keep wolves where I come from," Perceval said. "Why should I fear a sneaking dog? Be on your guard!"

The gilded knight gestured behind Perceval, where the road ran over the crest of the hill. "Run home, boy, and send one of those knights on the hill to fight me. I see the bars of Lancelot, and I did not dare this adventure to fight with such as you."

Perceval did not spare a glance over his shoulder, but he breathed slowly once to calm the fire in his belly. So if he died here today, the pale Queen had other avengers. And if he lived, his victory had witnesses. He took a dart, balancing it in his hand, choosing it with as much care as his next words. "Buckle to fight," he said. "If I allow it, you may yet live to boast of the day you met Perceval of Wales."

Within his helm, the knight snorted in derision.

"Besides, I go in need of arms, and I mean not to leave without yours."

"I should only dishonour my blade on you, boy."

"No fear of that," said Perceval, and grinned. "You have seen to that already."

The knight spurred his horse forward suddenly and swiped at Perceval's head with his spear-butt. Perceval ducked, and the blow fell on his left shoulder, momentarily numbing the arm. He forced a laugh.

"I only ever allowed my mother to beat me," he said, "and even she could hit harder than that!"

His enemy drew back up the hill, set his spear in rest, and came thundering down toward Perceval. The spear passed through empty air, for Perceval slid aside and down and clung to his dozing pony with just one arm and leg thrown athwart the back.

"Hah! You call yourself a knight!" he mocked, pulling himself upright. "First you go to spear an unarmed man, and then you run away down the hillside!"

The knight kicked his horse around and drew his sword, galloping back up the hill. Perceval waited for his chance. The distance between him and the knight closed to only a few yards before he lifted and flicked his arm. The dart flew true, striking home in the slit of the knight's visor.

The dead man toppled backward and fell to the ground at Llech's feet. With a snort, the pony awoke.

Perceval slipped to the ground, kicked the sword away from the body, yanked out his dart, and knelt to listen at the visor slit for breath. There was not a sound. Opening the knight's wallet, he found the Queen's cup and set it carefully in the grass by the road. Then he began to tap at the joints of the armour, and managed to slide off one of the knight's gauntlets. He glanced up the hill, wishing that the two knights on the crest would come and help him, but they had ridden after the dead man's horse.

Perceval unclasped the knight's belt and sword, and laid them in the road. He pulled off the wine-coloured surcoat and began searching for an opening in the mail. There was a leather lacing at the neck, where the helm was attached, and when he undid it and lifted the helm he saw the face of the man he had killed—his eyeball a bleeding mess, his pale, sweat-streaked face looking idiotically surprised. It was not the first time Perceval had killed a man, but it was the first time he had had to disarm a body. He thought of pulling the knight through the gorget, but the effort was obviously useless. He sat back, trying not to retch.

There was only one thing he could think of—fire. He scraped up a pile of tinder and took a flint from his pouch.

At that moment he heard the clatter of hooves and looked up to see the two knights who had followed him, Lancelot who bore red bars on a field of white, and the one named Gawain, whose sign was a five-pointed golden star.

"What are you doing now, boy?" asked the knight of the star.

"He is dead," said Perceval, working at the flint. "And I need his armour."

"And the fire?"

"Out of the iron, burn the tree," said Perceval, quoting a saying of his mother's.

Sir Gawain laughed. "There is no need to burn the man," he said, dismounting. "Let me show you."

34

He showed Perceval how to unlace the armour and draw it off, and with Sir Lancelot's help armed him, belted on the sword, and put shield and lance into his hands.

"Will you return to Camelot?" Sir Lancelot asked.

"Not today, sir," said Perceval. "Take the Queen's cup back to her. Tell her how I avenged the insult, and tell the chieftain of Britain how I bore his trust. But I will not go back myself until I have proved myself in a better fashion, with knightly weapons."

"You have proved yourself well enough," said Gawain. "If you will not come back to Camelot, let me knight you now."

So Sir Gawain knighted Perceval there on the road, and the two knights took the Queen's cup and left him. But Sir Perceval rode away into the forest, leading Llech with the bundle of skins and darts strapped to his back.

He rode north and west, choosing the loneliest paths, and at sunset he came to a castle on a green lawn beside a lake bathed in golden light. On the lawn an old grey-haired man stood watching a group of boys shooting with arrows at a mark. To him Perceval approached and said, "May I lie here tonight? I am weary, and have travelled far."

"Surely you may," said the old man, "and longer, if you will. What is your errand in this country?"

"I am a new-made knight," said Perceval. "But I have never used arms before, and so I am riding out to find some adventure on which to test them."

The old man laughed. "You had best stay awhile with me, and learn the use of them first," he said. "Come! It is long since I trained a knight, but I remember the old art well."

Chapter 4

I was afeared of her face though she fair were,
And said, "Mercy, Madame, what is this to mean?"
Langland

BLANCHE WAS STILL STARING AT THE red-gold ring when she went downstairs to the dining-room and found Nerys making tea. The girl was wearing quiet grey and her raven hair was pinned up at the nape of her neck: surely, thought Blanche, the unearthly beauty that had been hers in the dream of the pavilion could not have shone from this meek shadow. The contrast was so strong and sudden that Blanche slid the ring back onto her finger, sure now that she had been mistaken and the ring had been red all along. She would say nothing.

At breakfast Sir Ector said "Good morning" absent-mindedly, and if he had noticed the change in the ring—or that she was wearing a ring at all—he did not say. After the meal, Blanche went upstairs to wrestle with the *Aeneid*. Sir Ector had insisted she learn Latin when she was small, and still expected her to construe a hundred lines or so every day, although he allowed her to choose her reading.

It was while fumbling with a particularly difficult line that Blanche's mind began to wander and she remembered the inscription that had been in the ring Sir Ector had given her last night. *Guinevere, chaste and true.* She tugged once at the gold ring before the awful truth hit her and she looked down at it again with her stomach quaking.

She could not have dreamed that talk in the library. She could not have dreamed the inscription, and if it was not on this ring, then this was a different ring and sometime during the night, in who knows what place or time, a ring had been taken from her finger and replaced.

She touched her mouth. Her breath shivered against cold fingers.

Slowly, Blanche drew the ring from her finger. She sat there a moment longer, holding the heavy jewel without looking at it. Then she turned it and saw—nothing. No words spidered within the band.

Blanche sat in her chair a moment longer, thinking. Then, quite calmly, she rose from the desk and went—her feet soundless as the dream of the meadow—downstairs to the library.

The door stood ajar. She lifted her hand and laid it on the door, but could not for a moment gather the courage to push it open.

Then she heard Nerys speaking in a soft and urgent staccato: "But the time is growing short. That was Nimue's message. Again, and more often, I hear a rumour on the night airs—"

"She isn't ready, Nerys."

Ready for what? Blanche strained her ears over the thump of her own heart and the muffled protests of conscience. Nerys said: "I know. But how long have we already waited?"

Sir Ector did not reply and for one brief moment Blanche heard the shushing murmur of Nerys's skirts. When she spoke again, it was in Welsh, and there was an odd cadence in her voice:

"Sir, I have not the wit nor craft to know what might be coming upon us, or from which quarter. But be sure that either it is coming, or it is already here. And this place will not shield us when it comes."

Blanche blinked at the dim-pale shadow of her hand spread out across the massy oak panels of the library door. What was coming?

Suddenly the door twitched away from under her hand. Light struck her in the face and she looked into Nerys's eyes with a guilty start.

Nerys said nothing and Blanche could detect no sign of contempt in her expression. But even a scolding would have been easier to bear than that level unblinking gaze. Blanche flushed painfully and stammered. "I—I—"

Sir Ector came to her rescue. "Blanche, my dear, come in."

Nerys moved aside. With another start Blanche remembered why she had come. She went forward to her guardian's desk, put the red-gold ring down on the blotter, and looked up at Sir Ector as if hoping that he would explain the change in such a way that she could go on believing that this safe corner of the world so shrouded in comfort was the waking, and that the adventure in the pavilion and the dread in Nerys's voice was the dream.

"What does it mean?" she said. "What am I unready for? What is coming?"

Sir Ector lifted his hand to his beard and tugged on it with an odd gesture of helplessness. He looked at Nerys.

"You tell her, damsel."

"Damsel," repeated Blanche, and her stomach grew a little

colder.

Nerys took both Blanche's hands and led her to a chair. "Some wine," she said over her shoulder to Sir Ector. Then, with a sympathy that shone from every look and word like a lantern on a cold night, she said, "How long have we known each other, Blanche?"

Blanche swallowed. "Years. Always."

"And you know you can trust me."

She nodded.

"How old am I, Blanche?"

Sir Ector came with a glass of port. Already her mind was beginning to work again, but Blanche took a velvet-sweet sip before replying. "About my age, aren't you?"

"Do you remember how, years ago, I taught you to read? How old was I then?"

Blanche felt another stabbing chill. "You were already grown-up." She stared into her governess-companion's face. "Nerys. It's been fourteen years and you haven't aged."

"No." Nerys settled back on her footstool, her shoulders falling, her chin lifting. For a moment the veil rose: Blanche sensed a dignity so awful and majestic that she almost expected the footstool to splinter into diamond shards beneath its burden.

"I am ageless."

"I never noticed," said Blanche in a dry mouth.

Nerys shimmered in amusement. "No."

"How could I never have noticed? Is it magic?"

"It is natural. For me."

Under her eyes, the ageless woman folded back into herself and the glimpse of glory was gone. Blanche was glad, for under its weight she had felt too small for her own comfort. But once seen, the thing was not to be forgotten or brushed from mind. Blanche drank some more port and stared at the carpet. It was no use, she thought. She was in the dreamworld now.

She looked up tiredly and pointed to the ring on the blotter. "The ring. The boy. The pavilion. It was all real. …My mother, Guinevere." She turned to Sir Ector. "I said—I said, 'Who was my father, Arthur, King of the Britons?' I was *joking*."

Sir Ector and Nerys looked at her, and their solemnity, like a wall of marble, threw her doubt back in her face.

Blanche gasped for breath.

"That's why you're an antiquary, Sir Ector. You're not fascinated by the ancients, you *are* an ancient. L'Espée. The Swordsman."

A smile hovered on his lips. "Keep going, Blanche. You're doing well."

She shook her head, drained of words, and covered her face with her hands. Sir Ector laid a comforting hand on her shoulder. Blanche snatched uselessly at her whirling thoughts for a moment before she remembered what she had overheard.

"Nerys. You said something was coming."

"Yes…" Once more, Nerys answered obliquely. "When you were born, eighteen years ago in Logres, the King sent Sir Ector to Broceliande."

Sir Ector said: "In that tangled forest, in an enchanted tower by a hawthorn bush, the magician Merlin slumbers until the end of the world. When the Lord Arthur was a boy Merlin counselled and guided him, but when the King became a man, Merlin departed and no mortal man has seen him since—although, perhaps, he is seen by the Lady of the Lake and her people." And the knight glanced at Nerys.

"I rode many days before I found the Lady Nimue, and when

she heard my quest she agreed to take me to the tower. I saw not a stone of it. But when I asked, a voice came which I knew like my own brother's. 'Pendragon's heir is the life of Logres.' "

Nerys said: "Therefore the Lady my mistress knew that your life would be in danger."

Blanche stared at her. "Danger from whom?"

"From all those who hate Logres."

She shook her head helplessly. "I don't know what that is."

Sir Ector gestured. "The Pendragon is your father—it's the title borne by the High King of Britain. Arthur is the Pendragon by election and conquest and the divine will of the High King of all kings. His realm is Logres, of which Camelot is the capital."

"The Pendragon has many enemies," Nerys went on, "and his sister Morgan le Fay had already tried to destroy him. He is not a man to spend a thought on his own danger, but even he saw that you could not live safely in Logres. By the gates of my people you were carried across the gulf of worlds to another place, a world where the sorceress Morgan could not find you, a world where you—and the life of Logres—would be safe."

"But you said time was running out."

Sir Ector leaned against his desk, folding his arms. "Blanche, this is what we have been trying to prepare you for all these years. You do not belong in this world. One day you must return to Logres for good and take your rightful place."

"And it will be soon, Blanche," Nerys added.

It was too much to think about. Blanche got up and took the gold ring from the blotter. "Who was he, Nerys, the boy in the pavilion?"

"His name is Perceval of Wales. By the account of my mistress, Nimue, he was going to Camelot to be made a knight."

"That savage, a knight?"

41

"There were prophecies at *his* birth, too."

Blanche frowned at the implied rebuke and looked at the ring. He is still a savage, she thought. "Will I see him again?"

"It is likely."

"Good!" Blanche flashed. "Prophecies or not, I shall box his ears." She thrust the gold band onto her finger. Then, as quickly as the spark had flared, it died away and suddenly she was exhausted, almost fighting back tears. "Was there anything else I should know?"

Sir Ector shook his head. "A hundred things. We need not speak of them now."

Blanche nodded and went toward the door. On the threshold, she looked back and saw Sir Ector and Nerys still sitting where she had left them, staring into another time. She cleared her throat.

"Thank you for telling me the truth," she said very softly, and went away.

SHE WAS SITTING IN HER WINDOW-SEAT staring out at the rain when a tap sounded at the door and Nerys entered. She moved swiftly over to the window, concern in her voice.

"Will you weather this, Blanche?"

Blanche nodded.

Nerys glanced out the window at the colourless grey sky and sank onto the window-seat. "You will have questions, I imagine."

Blanche looked at her clasped hands and tightened her lips. There was a small hard knot of resentment under her breastbone, and it did not want to ask any questions, or learn any more about the place Nerys called Logres.

"How can you be sure," she ventured at last, "that Merlin was referring to me?"

Nerys's eyelash flickered. She glanced sidelong at Blanche, and Blanche knew that she had hit something, there.

Nerys said, "He spoke of the Pendragon's heir."

Blanche looked back down at her twined hands. "And I am the Pendragon's daughter? When I asked Sir Ector last night, he did not seem so sure." And she held her breath, almost afraid of what Nerys might say to that.

Her answer came quickly, lightly: "It's only talk, Blanche."

"So there's talk...It's about my mother and—that other knight. Lancelot, isn't it?"

Nerys sighed. "Gossip a thousand years old and more, in the French romances. Blanche, it's true that when you were born, every malicious tongue was clacking, but..."

"Nerys, you don't seem sure yourself."

A pause.

"And I am unsure, but for no good reason." Nerys rose to her feet and paced the room, eyebrows stitched together. "The Queen claimed you were true-born—"

"Claimed?"

"How should I know if the White Shadow of Cameliard was lying? I only know that no one believed her—save the King, of course—and sometimes, I thought she intended them not to. But only God knows why, for if the Queen had betrayed the King, it would be the ruin of Logres."

Blanche was silent for a while. Then she said:

"If I am not true-born then I need not return to Britain. And I will be safe, for my life will mean nothing to Logres or its enemies."

"Not return to Britain?" Nerys turned on her in blank surprise. "But it's your home."

43

"Is it?" Blanche looked around the cosy room that was her own. "*I* never saw it."

Nerys looked at her, shoulders slumping a little. "It is where your heritage lies. A patrimony for which men have killed and died, suffered exile and sorrow and counted the price little. ...I thought you might have been less indifferent to it. Or can it be that you are afraid of these enemies?"

Blanche coloured under her gaze. "Of course not," she said. But it was impossible now to keep the resentment out of her voice, for she knew she was lying.

ON SUNDAY, BLANCHE WENT WITH KITTY Walker's party to Tintern in a sour mood that was only fretted by the idle and carefree chatter of the others. But it was better than being trapped in the house with Sir Ector and Nerys, she thought to herself, and besides, she wanted to see Mr Corbin.

She took her chance when they reached Tintern, lagging behind Kitty and the two others as if she took some deep interest in the empty roof and lonely arches of the ruined abbey. Mr Corbin, as a matter of course, remained with her, looming on her left hand like some gigantic but melancholy bird. His silent presence, and the peacefulness of the grass-floored abbey, made it easier to let go some of the tension she had hidden with difficulty in the motor-car.

"Do you think it is more beautiful ruined than it might have been whole?" Mr Corbin asked presently.

Blanche tilted back her head to admire the delicate tracery of the great west window. All the glass was gone, of course, but the lingering gracefulness of the blind stone outline made the breath catch in her throat.

"My guardian would like it whole," she said at last, with a

bitter laugh. "I think he would prefer it if we all lived in castles."

"Ah," said Mr Corbin, "but think how chilly and dark that would be. Can't you imagine all the monks, like brown mice, shivering in here of a winter morning?" And he sang a bar or two of the *Te Deum* with an exaggerated vibrato.

Blanche tried to smile.

Laughter echoed from the walls as Kitty and her friends came tripping back to them. "Blanche," Kitty called, "we have seen it all, and we are going into the village to find a tea-shop. Are you coming?"

"I had rather stay a little longer," she told them, and they giggled knowingly as they went away.

She and Mr Corbin walked on, further into the abbey. She felt his eyes on her when they should have been on the ruin; she was not surprised when at last he said:

"You are quiet today, Miss Pendragon. Is anything troubling you?"

The mockery that lived in his eyes was gone for the moment, and Blanche let some of her distress show in her face.

"You would only laugh," she said helplessly.

"Try me."

Blanche shook her head. "You don't believe in things like this."

"Anything that worries you is real enough to concern me." He bent head and eyebrows to look into her face. "Look at me, Blanche. Can't you trust me?"

She searched his eyes in a wordless hush more intimate than speech. Before long she dropped her gaze to the grass beneath their feet. "My parents," she began at last.

His silence encouraged her to go on.

"All my life I thought they were dead. Now I find that they are alive, but so far away… I don't know what to do." She looked up, but he was still silent. "My guardian says I should go to them."

"They are a long way away?"

Blanche nodded, afraid to say anything more.

"And—you?"

"I suppose I must go…"

Mr Corbin smiled. "Miss Pendragon, how can I help you if you speak of *musts?*"

She looked up at him with quick hope. "What do you mean?"

Again the silence bore that odd secrecy, before he replied, "Whoever made a decision because of what *must* be done? Ask, rather, what you truly desire."

She looked into the sky and the sun was smiling. "A decision? You mean—I could say *no?*"

"Why not? If it is what you truly desire—on your own account."

Blanche gulped. But she was unsurprised by the thought, for it had been lurking at the back of her mind until liberated by Mr Corbin's words. Sudden tears rose in her throat and she blurted out:

"I can't go! I *can't!* It would kill me!"

She stared up at him, blinking back the tears. He took her arm with a swift gesture of comfort. "But this is melodrama, Blanche. How far away can they be? Paris? Milan?"

The mention of those two kindly cities struck her as a cruel joke. "Oh, if only!"

"India, then? But that isn't far. Not today. Haven't you read that capital book, by Mr Verne, wasn't it?"

"It isn't India," she said.

He frowned. "Surely not Australia?"

46

In the midst of her tragedy she couldn't help laughing. "No, indeed!"

But Mr Corbin remained serious. "You said I wouldn't believe you, Blanche. What aren't you telling me?"

"You would laugh…"

"I give you my word not to laugh. Tell me, Blanche. Better than keeping it all bottled up inside."

Blanche screwed her eyes shut. Then she said, "My mother is named Guinevere, and she is the one you are thinking of."

"THERE'S EVEN A PROPHECY," SHE FINISHED. "Pendragon's heir is the life of Logres. If I go back there, I'll be killed!" She glanced up at Mr Corbin's saturnine profile. "Oh, but you can't believe me. You don't believe in fairy-tales, do you?"

"I do not," he said. "But I know of science, and the strange properties of space and time. Why shouldn't this all be possible?"

Blanche gaped. "You mean you believe me?"

"Of course I do. You are not crazy, and why should you be lying?"

"You're *wonderful*," she cried. "Tell me, what should I do? This is my home—this time, this place. I don't want to leave."

Mr Corbin shrugged. "Your parents thought they were doing their best for you, sending you here. Who would willingly leave, having stood on the brink of the twentieth century and looked into a bright future where war and poverty might very well vanish, within fifteen years or so, before a peaceful brotherhood of humanity…? It is hard on you, having lived here, to go back to the Dark Ages." He glanced up at the abbey with a laugh. "Only just now I was speaking of the discomforts of such places."

47

"I shall probably have to live in something like it." Blanche felt tears crawling up her throat again. "Oh, what shall I do?"

Mr Corbin shook his head. "Miss Pendragon, you are not a child anymore. Nobody can advise you, least of all me. You must follow your own heart and judgement."

She looked at him in doubt. "I've always done what Sir Ector advised. Or Nerys. They always knew best. And I know they love me. How could I disappoint them?"

"But everyone makes mistakes," he said gently. "Especially with their children, I think; they are so full of their own hopes that they forget to let you have yours. Don't be afraid to know your own mind."

Blanche nodded, and let her gaze fall to her feet. "I will try. I will try to make the right choice."

"Miss—Blanche," said Mr Corbin, and stepped closer. She shivered with surprise as his cool fingers tipped her chin. She looked up, into his eyes, and smiled awkwardly; after the adventure of the pavilion, she felt shy even of Mr Corbin. But he returned the smile, and her discomfort smoothed away.

"The only wrong choice," he told her with gentle insistence, "would be to let someone else choose for you."

Chapter 5

Nay, then,
Do what thou canst, I will not go to-day;
No, nor to-morrow, not till I please myself.
Shakespeare

IT WAS A WARM MAY EVENING not long after the excursion to Tintern, and Blanche sat on the hammock in the garden. She had been reading a Miss Austen novel, *Mansfield Park*, but even the charming Crawfords no longer distracted her thoughts, and she had flung the book down among the cushions. Instead she was tatting lace for a collar, her fingers scrambling wildly across the cotton. The sun, sinking into flaming clouds, would be gone soon and the bite of cold would send her indoors, to dinner and Nerys and polite conversation. Blanche tatted a little faster. She needed to *think*.

The shuttle, followed by its inky shadow, danced up and down above the cream-coloured lace and Blanche, staring through it, still saw the windows of Tintern. Since the trip she had not spoken to anyone about what she had learned from Nerys and Sir Ector in the library. If anything, she had tried to forget. But her time was running out. Her guardian would return in a day or two from the Newport Antiquities Society's monthly meeting, and when he spoke to her about it again—as he certainly would soon—she needed to have a decision.

But what decision? "Don't be afraid to know your own mind," Mr Corbin had said. Blanche felt like laughing. Know her own mind! It was easy for him to say it, but her mind fought knowing. Mr Corbin was right, of course: it was hard, it was *impossible* for her to leave this time willingly, with everything that she knew and loved. But Sir Ector and Nerys expected her to go—expected her to return to take up the life to which she had been born and even, in a way, raised. How would she ever talk them into letting her stay? She stirred uncomfortably in her seat.

She heard a door close and looked across a lawn like green fire to see Nerys coming from the house to call her for dinner. The sun flared once and was swallowed up in a velvet bank of cloud. The light changed from gold to purple. Red bled across the horizon and Blanche, suddenly in shadow, rose from the hammock. Then she shivered in a breath of wind that scattered the perfume of roses and sent a dank, earthy scent fluttering around her.

She pulled her shawl closer. The wind raced across the lawn and tugged loose the strands of Nerys's hair. For a moment, apart from the leaves and grasses stirred by that chill breath, all motion ceased. Blanche saw her draw breath. Then the gust died and Nerys was hurrying across the lawn calling her name.

"Blanche—come quickly."

Blanche dug among the cushions for her book and thrust it with the tatting into her work-basket. As she fumbled with the catch, Nerys caught her arm. "Leave it," she panted. At the uneven note in her voice, Blanche turned and looked at her. Something of the immortal woman's glory had broken loose with the strands of hair, some hint of power hung about her, but her eyes were wide with what could only be called fear. Blanche dropped her work-basket.

Then Nerys's fingers gripped Blanche's arm convulsively, and her gaze slid past, into the shadows of the bushes beyond. Blanche turned to see. For a moment she saw nothing; then the shadows coalesced. There, just beyond the beeches from which the hammock hung, stood the statue of a man in armour, shield on arm, sword drawn.

Blanche felt the hair rise along the back of her neck. The weird light of dusk, the trembling of Nerys—*Nerys, trembling!*—and above all the mute, inexplicable figure reminded her of a childish nightmare. For one horrible moment she supposed that it must have been standing there watching her for hours. But it moved, and was an armoured man with a sword coming at them around the tree.

Blanche screamed before she could stop herself. Then Nerys snatched her hand and they were fleeing across the lawn to the house. Footsteps pounded behind them. Blanche did not dare to look over her shoulder. They reached the door and flung against it. Blanche grabbed blindly for the knob; then the door spilled them into the hall.

She looked back. Nerys was there, almost stumbling into her arms; behind Nerys, the knight and the sword, only yards away and closing in. "Quickly—the wardrobe," Nerys said, slamming the door shut, and shooting the bolt.

At the foot of the stairs, in the middle of the house, stood a wardrobe which Blanche knew had nothing in it but coats and tennis-racquets, though it was always kept locked. Was it like Nerys's wardrobe upstairs? Would it take them to safety? She darted down the hall and tugged the handle. Then a heavy blow struck the back-door and shook the whole house. There was such implacable malice in the shivering air that Blanche nearly screamed again. Nerys pushed her aside, fumbling at a chain around her neck.

Voices and running feet came up the passage from the kitchen. One of the housemaids looked into the hall just as another violent crash shook the house. The bolt on the door was not a heavy one. Already the bar was bending and the wood of the door was splintering. But Nerys, poised with a key in her hand, said calmly to the maid:

"Tell Keats we shall be a few minutes late for dinner, will you, Lucy?"

Whether it was Nerys's cool manner, or some exertion of that veiled authority, Blanche never knew. The girl nodded and disappeared. Nerys fitted the key into the wardrobe lock and turned it. With a jerk, she pulled the door open a crack, and stood waiting.

"What are you doing?" Blanche gasped.

Nerys lifted a finger.

The next blow came accompanied by the sound of splitting wood. Then with one more crash the door burst off its hinges into the hall. Blanche drew a breath like a sob. The knight stepped over the threshold toward them, silhouetted against angry twilight. Nerys, pale and concentrated, whisked open the wardrobe door and swept Blanche inside.

BLANCHE STUMBLED INTO IRON-GREY RAIN SLASH-ING down from a clouded mid-afternoon sky. She stood in the stony courtyard of a castle, empty except for three posts standing erect by the wall and a man holding a sword. She blinked and gasped under the battering rain.

52

The man in the courtyard straightened and turned to her, sweeping rain and sweat from his eyes. Blanche, reeling toward him, looked into his face and saw recognition. The boy from the pavilion.

In that moment of terror she remembered that meeting only as something insignificant and long ago. She only saw his lean whiplike strength, the sword in his hand, and the eyes that had always been honest. "Please," she gasped, glancing past Nerys, behind her, to the low stable door she had somehow exited, "help."

As she said the word the door wrenched open and their pursuer came out into the rain. She had forgotten to speak Welsh, but her panic spoke for her. Perceval glanced from the terrified women to the knight—immense, armoured *cap-a-pie*, with a two-handed sword that made his own feel like a toy—and laughed, more from the unexpectedness of the thing than anything else.

"Stand behind me," he said to the flame-haired damsel, and as she and her attendant darted out of the way he raised his shield, lifted his sword to shoulder height, and crouched low.

The strange knight spoke, his voice echoing inside the iron helm. "Do you seek death, boy?"

Perceval grinned. "I've yanked his beard once or twice. I can do it again."

Something stirred beneath the massive iron plates of the knight's armour—something that may have been a shrug. Then the great sword lifted like the blade of a guillotine: two steps forward, and a rain of blows fell upon Perceval, who staggered back just too late and fell to one knee, lifting a smashed shield on a senseless arm to receive a new attack. Blanche gasped; at any moment she expected to see the boy crumple like blotting-

53

paper. But then he lashed out at the knight's knee and somehow reeled to his feet out of the enemy's reach.

The two circled in the rain with quick, taut steps. Blanche and Nerys, clinging together, shuffled to stay behind the boy. The knight lunged; there was a flash of steel like lightning and the fierce shriek of metal. Perceval maneuvered again, and Blanche found that she and Nerys were standing before the stable door.

On the other side of Perceval the enemy knight had also seen this, and Blanche flinched again as he burst into deadly motion. But Nerys, tugging her arm with white fingers, hissed in her ear. "Now!"

Blanche resisted for a moment. "Can't we do something?" she groaned under the screech and crash of swords.

"We can run!"

Nerys pulled her toward the stable door. Blanche glanced back and what she saw remained frozen like a photograph in her mind long afterwards: two swords crossed in the air, and the planted feet and straining arms of both combatants. There was blood, mixed with rain, flowing down the boy's shield arm. Then she was in the hallway of her own home again, dripping rain from an afternoon far away. Nerys slammed the wardrobe door and locked it, and even the dim light which shone from the keyhole had vanished when she removed the key.

Nerys leaned back against the wardrobe, closed her eyes, and took a deep, trembling breath.

Blanche's legs buckled and she slid down the wall to the floor. She hugged her knees and breathed for a moment. "H-he can't come back?"

"Not at present."

"And the boy?" The boy in the pavilion, who had frightened

her and robbed her. Again in her mind Blanche saw blood running down the young knight's shield arm and with dispassionate wonder realised that somewhere in the last few breathless seconds, she had forgiven him. "Will he live?"

Nerys opened her eyes, her voice matter-of-fact. "I cannot tell."

Blanche swallowed. "He'll be killed!"

"It's possible," said Nerys. "But not, I think, probable. The sons of Orkney are made of sterner stuff than the brigands of Gore."

AN AGE AWAY IN THE RAIN, Perceval heard the door slam behind him, and at that distracted moment his enemy disengaged. The next stroke caught the broken shield on his arm, scooped him aside, and flung him to the cobblestones. His enemy did not pursue the advantage, however. Instead he threw open the door of the stable and stood motionless, staring into the warm questioning eyes of horses.

In the sudden silence, there were shouts from within the castle and men-at-arms spilled into the courtyard.

The knight fell back a step and breathed out a curse, looking at Perceval.

"Do not doubt that this debt will be repaid with interest." And he strode into the stable.

BLANCHE SHOOK HER HEAD, A WAVE of dizzy tiredness sweeping over her. "Nerys, I don't understand. How did this happen?"

Nerys looked at her with quick compassion. "The thing we feared," she said. "She has found you at last: Morgan le Fay, the Queen of Gore."

"The sorceress? But who was the knight?"

"Did you not mark his shield?"

Blanche gave a barking laugh. "I did not!"

Nerys shook her head. "I forget that to you, a shield is not the same as a placard. He bore the Blue Boar, the device of Sir Odiar, the Queen's paramour and cutthroat."

PERCEVAL STRUGGLED TO HIS FEET AND reeled toward the stable door. Just as he reached it, a screaming neigh warned him to dive aside. Even so, the rush of horseflesh that broke open the door almost swept him away. All the horses of the castle spilled into the courtyard at once, and in the midst of them the knight of Gore, riding easily without saddle or bit, raced them across the courtyard, burst open the closing gate, trampled down the rising drawbridge, and was gone.

In the lull that followed a cool silence and numbness fell on Perceval. His knees gave way and he sank to the threshold of the stable, cradling his gashed shield arm. Dimly, in the background, he heard the roar of flames.

"AND THIS?" BLANCHE GESTURED TO THE wardrobe. "It goes back to Logres?"

"Yes." Nerys laid her hand on it. "When I knew that Sir Ector would be gone, I bound the key to the Castle Gornemant so that if there was need we could go to Sir Perceval. Not that I imagined we would need it." Her brows knitted. "How much does Morgan know? She could not have chosen a better moment for an attack. Did she know Sir Ector was away?"

A drip of ancient water ran down Blanche's neck, but the shiver tingling her spine felt more like fear. "What now?"

Nerys shook her head. "If the Queen of Gore has found you,

the best I can do is hold the walls for a while. Sooner or later she will find her way back."

Blanche swallowed. "You mean that I'll be sent back to Logres."

"We knew the time was coming," Nerys reminded her.

In the sudden relief of escape, Blanche could no longer hold back the words.

"I don't want to leave. I don't want to live in that place. The very thought of it makes me feel sick. Nerys, I'm so sorry, but I just *can't*."

Chapter 6

See ye not the narrow road
By yon lillie leven?
That's the road the righteous goes
And that's the road to heaven.
The Queen of Elfland's Nourice

IN THE SILENCE AFTER BLANCHE'S WORDS Nerys went down the hallway to the smashed door and stood silhouetted against the last purple and yellow streaks of sunset, risen up on tiptoe with her chin lifted as though sniffing or listening. At last she turned.

"Come with me."

She plunged out the door and Blanche ran to catch up with her. Outside, a cold gale whipped through the trees, tumbling leaves and twigs across the lawn toward the house. Already the rose-bushes by the hammock were stripped of their petals. Beyond, in the orchard, the apple-trees creaked and groaned: the blast almost seemed stronger here. It whipped hair into her face and blinded her, and in that dizzy moment the gale seemed the wind of an incredible speed, as though she was rushing through a tunnel on the viewing-platform of a train. Then, unsettled and breathless, she pushed her hair back and struggled after Nerys.

The gate at the end of the orchard was open, with a snapped latch and one broken hinge. Nerys wrestled it upright and flung all her weight against it.

"Help me," she called back. The wind snatched the words from her mouth, but Blanche understood the sense, if not the purpose, and threw herself against the gate. They strained in the teeth of the wind for a few gasping seconds. Then the gate closed, and the wind was gone.

Nerys, catlike, smoothed hair and skirts before gesturing to the gate.

"Look at this. Brute force. A hole blown open between the worlds."

Blanche stared. "Is that where *he* got in?"

"Yes," said Nerys. "Feel it." She took Blanche's hand and held it to the broken latch of the gate where a cold jet of air still whistled through. "That woman has done damage to the very weft of the world. If you opened that gate and walked through, you would be in Logres. And if anyone there knows about this…"

"Morgan knows," Blanche whispered. "What are we going to do?"

Again Nerys looked at her with inexpressible sympathy. "It might frighten you to think of living in Logres, Blanche, but all our defences are thrown down in this world. Logres is the safest place for you now."

She turned back to the house, walking quickly, and continued.

"They won't think to look for you in Britain. We'll telegraph Sir Ector and tell the servants you've been called suddenly away. Pack light, for we haven't a moment to spare, and we may have far to travel. I don't know how far it is to Camelot from the Castle Gornemant."

To Camelot. Now. Already. Blanche, choking down her dismay, caught Nerys's arm. "But we'll come back, won't we?"

Nerys sighed and shook her head. "I know this is sudden, Blanche. Only believe me when I say that you are in deadly danger now, every moment, until we have you back in Camelot. Sir Ector and I can close up the house, mend the rift, and say goodbye to the neighbours. There is no point in exposing you to the danger of another journey."

Blanche felt helpless—a cold dull panic which she was beginning to recognise. "Mr Corbin," she said. "I want to say goodbye. Kitty, too, and Emmeline. I can't just disappear. How will you explain it to them if I do? They'll have to be told *something*."

Nerys stopped walking and looked at her. "Blanche," she said, and despite the gentleness of her words Blanche knew she was vexed, "do you really mean to put your friends above your own safety and the future of Logres?" A pause. "The decision does not rest with me, at any rate. Gather your things."

When Blanche came downstairs with her bag she found Nerys already waiting by the wardrobe, key in hand. She had thought of another objection.

"What if that knight is still on the other side? The one with the Blue Boar?"

"Odiar loves not the company of true and faithful men like Gornemant," Nerys said. "He will be fled or captured by now. Stand back."

But when she fitted the key to the lock and turned it, there was a sudden muted roar and the door fought like a wild thing against Nerys's hand. Through the narrow opening yellow flames shot out into the hallway, singing Nerys's hair and licking the wallpaper. She said "Ah," slammed the door shut, and turned the key again.

"*Heavens!*" Blanche cried, staring at the buckled and blistered door.

"The door is on fire," Nerys said. "And the key can only be linked to another door from the Logres side."

"We can't leave?" Blanche looked hopeful.

"We can and we must. We'll go out through the orchard."

"But Morgan is on the other side!"

Nerys went to the doorway again and sniffed the night air. "Such damage is not done in a chamber. She would have done it in the open. Also it is raining in Britain. If we take the horses, we may slip through without being seen and ride away without being caught."

"Are you positive it wouldn't be safer to stay here?"

"Waiting to be attacked at any moment? Or leading the hounds of Gore a merry chase around Gloucestershire?"

Blanche bit her lip. For all Mr Corbin's insistence that she make her own choices, it looked as if she would be forced into Logres, for refuge if nothing else.

"We must go on, and take the adventure that comes." Nerys went out the door toward the stable, and there was nothing to do but follow.

FLORENCE WAS BLANCHE'S HORSE, AN UNINTELLI-GENT but sweet-tempered bay. Nerys, who did not have a horse of her own, had taken Sir Ector's, a retrained grey racer named Malaventure. The pair of them pricked their ears and swished their tails in the face of the wind between the worlds. Blanche fidgeted with the reins.

Nerys had already gone, taking with her a windfall apple. "If all is well, I'll throw the apple back through the gate, and you'll know it is safe to bring the horses. If not, *ride*."

Then she had stepped through the gate. The quick-falling dusk made it difficult to see what happened next. Only Blanche had blinked, and Nerys was gone.

Deep inside she was panicking again, fearing that the worst must have happened when the apple landed with a *plop* on the grass at her feet. Then, without a pause to let herself think, she clucked to the horses and plunged into the wind, dragging at their reins.

It was dark beyond the gate, and again she felt that sense of limitless speed. Soon the wind lashing her face had water in it, and as the rain grew heavier, the wind died away and under shadowy oaks Blanche looked down to see that she was standing in a circle of blackened stones. Hurriedly she stepped out of it, with low calm words for the skittish horses.

No one was to be seen. Away to the right the trees thinned and the towers of a castle could be glimpsed rising out of the clearing, black against the dark evening sky. At the sight, Blanche's scalp prickled and the blood hummed in her ears. She was engulfed, quite without expecting it, in a high and dauntless mood. Here she stood under weeping skies, she, Blanche Pendragon, who bore a name of legend. In that castle, all unaware, lay a witch-queen who desired her death, and echoing in the back of her mind she could still hear the fierce steel voices of swords, harsher and sweeter and wilder in her veins than any other sound on the green earth. And she had been caught and kissed by a brown boy from the woods, and he had paid for the pleasure in blood.

For one titanic heartbeat she felt as tall as the trees.

Then above her a shadow rose with a sound like the tearing of cloth and her heart leaped into her throat before she saw that it was only a black bird beating the air with sharp pinions. The trees bent down over her again, and it was night in Logres and very cold in the rain. Blanche ducked her head and turned up the collar of her jacket. Not until then did she see Nerys coming toward her through the trees from the direction of the castle with a finger lifted to her lips.

Nerys shoved Malaventure's hindquarters away from the stone circle on the ground. This she unmade, moving with an queer and wordless vehemence. One by one she tore the stones out of the turf and flung them like missiles into the undergrowth. She was finished in a matter of moments and straightened, catching her breath. Then she swung into the saddle and led the way south through the soft murmur of rain.

Neither spoke until the castle was out of earshot. At last Nerys said:

"A raven was watching us as we came through."

"Yes, I saw."

Nerys pushed hair out of her eyes. "You saw, but did you understand? Some of the ravens are *her* creatures. In any case she will be on our trail by morning."

No need to ask who *she* was. But in a country where legends walked, what could go wrong?

"If she waits until morning to follow us, we'll leave her far behind."

"Unless she left a guard," said Nerys. "When she sees that the stone ring was destroyed, she will know we used her passage."

"Then why did you destroy it?"

"The keys to the doors between the worlds are ours to use—I and my people," Nerys said. "But Morgan le Fay is a mortal, and has no right to them. She must use unnatural force. Magic which I will have nothing to do with and destroy when I find it."

"You and your people?"

"The Fair Folk."

"You mean—fairies. Immortals like you." Blanche glanced sidelong at her companion, her fancy kindling. "Are there many of you in Britain?"

"Two or three, perhaps."

"So few?"

"My people are not of Logres. They have no concern here."

"But you do?" Blanche was puzzled.

Nerys was quiet for a time before replying. "All mortals die," she said at last. "All take the broad road to Hell, or the narrow road to Heaven. But my people do not die while the world endures. Therefore they spend their time doing what pleases themselves. They have no stake in the struggle between Logres and darkness."

"And you?"

"I cannot tell," she said with a sigh. "In the lore of my people it is said that we are outside salvation. But within the last hundred years I have heard differently. It was a wandering saint who told me that even the bonny road to Elfland comes to a fork in the end. If only it were true! If only there were hope for us."

Far in the distance behind them, a horn blew, a sound so lovely in the moonlight that a chill ran down Blanche's spine. Then came the bell of hounds and the cold settled lead-heavy in her stomach.

Nerys stiffened in the saddle. "The dogs. She knows."

Blanche glanced back. It was full night, now, and the rain

had stopped, leaving the moon swimming through cloud. Only a weak and fitful light filtered through the arching branches overhead. "We can ride faster, even in this dark."

"A little."

Nerys led them now slightly to the right and they pressed on into rough hill-country. Behind, at intervals, they heard the horn, and each time it drew closer. This slow cold hunt across the hills in fainting moonlight was worse even than the terror of the Blue Boar, Blanche thought, as they went down a rocky slope with the horses stumbling and slipping beneath them. And for one impious moment she wished to stand again in the shattered calm of the hallway at home with nowhere to run and the door splintering beneath the enemy's blows.

The moon was low in the sky when they stumbled into a bog between two towering hills.

Malaventure found ground on the other side of the slough, but Florence stuck fast, too weary to fight. Blanche dismounted and sank up to her knees in scummed water as cold as conceit. At that moment a breeze gusted from the north, carrying the noise of the hunt.

"Come *on*," Blanche begged. Florence wallowed and plunged, and Blanche lost her balance, stumbling into softer mud and deeper water. The cold gripped her thighs. She struggled back to higher ground with her skirt clinging to her legs, and began to rattle in the icy wind. Chill fingers ran down her cheeks as the tears spilled over.

Then Nerys was beside her carrying a scrubby bough from a dead bush on the bank, and Blanche was grateful for the dark that hid her cowardice.

"Shh, be calm," Nerys said to the horse. To Blanche she said, "We must throw down branches for her to step on."

Blanche scrubbed her woollen cuff across her eyes and splashed to the bank. She could hear the hounds crying. Were they already in view? She seized more twigs and branches and plunged back into the water. So Morgan wanted to kill her? Good. But she would not die whimpering.

Beyond all hope they extracted Florence from the bog, but the sound of the hunt was coming over the hill and the horses were stumbling with weariness.

"Mount again," said Nerys through the darkness. "They may yet lose our scent in the water."

They toiled on up the slope ahead, and had reached the rocky shoulder of the hill when the baying of hounds fell silent behind them. Blanche looked back and a gleam of moonlight showed dark shapes coursing to and fro on the far side of the slough.

"We've outfoxed them!" she said, and they turned the corner of the rocky outcrop and blundered into firelight.

The campfire under the rocks illuminated only one man, a wizened old creature with a beard that reached his knees. His mule lay in shelter, chewing stolidly, but the man himself stood leaning on his staff by the fire, watching the night.

At the sight Florence and Malaventure stopped of their own accord, their heads drooping, sensing, perhaps, the bewilderment of their riders. Blanche looked at Nerys and saw something like defeat in the line of her mouth. Her eyes prickled with tears again. What was this old man doing here, so far from any shelter?

The ancient shifted his weight and spoke.

"Nerys of the Folk," he said. "It's a cold night to be wandering in the wilds."

Nerys's voice was flat as she replied. "How do you know me?"

"And Blanchefleur, heir of Logres. Exalted company for my

66

poor fireside."

In the distance, the musical cry of a hound announced to his fellows that the scent was found. Blanche saw Nerys's back pull tight and knew that she had heard.

"Tell us your name, since you're so free with ours," said the fay fiercely.

"My name? That is no secret," said the old man. "I am Naciens."

A pause—a long pause, while the hounds behind them gave tongue. At last Nerys spoke again. "Naciens of Carbonek? I know the name. What brings you here?"

"The witch of Gore is on your trail," Naciens said. "You will find the Castle of Carbonek in the valley beneath us. She will not."

"Carbonek!" The word came out like a gasp, raw with desire. Blanche stared. But then Nerys's hands gripped the reins tighter, and she was herself again. "I am taking the damsel Blanchefleur to safety, to Camelot. I cannot risk losing her in a place beyond space and time."

Naciens shrugged. "Ride to Camelot, then!"

The sound of hunting-horns floated mockingly up the hill. Blanche set her teeth and shivered in the wind. Nerys did not change expression.

"Camelot is seven days' ride from here, with fresh horses and on the right paths," said Naciens more gently. "If you ride alone, Morgan will certainly catch you. If it is safety you need, nowhere is safer than Carbonek."

Nerys said: "If I leave her at Carbonek, what hope have I of finding her again?"

Naciens stroked his beard in silence before replying. "Carbonek is not lost to those to whom it is given to find," he said at last. "Or do you think that I myself have brought you through these hills to our doorstep in the nick of time? Tell me, have you forgotten what is kept there?"

Nerys bowed her head. And then Blanche thought she must have gone mad, for in the hush, below the ever-louder baying of hounds, she sang.

I have fled from the wilderness fasting, with woe and unflagging travail,
I have sought for the light on the mountain, and skirted the devilish dale.
I have laid my mouth in the dust, and begged the Might to be kind,
I have come to the feast, and I famish. Now grant me the Holy Grail.

Blanche stirred like a sleeper waking. Naciens was speaking.

"To you, it is given."

Chapter 7

But a lamp above a gate
Shone in solitary state,
O'er a desert drear and cold,
O'er a heap of ruins old,
O'er a scene most desolate.
Rossetti

Art thou, like Angels, only shown,
Then to our Grief for ever flown?
Heyrick

ONE DAY SIR PERCEVAL TOOK HIS horse and arms, both the spoils of the gilded knight, and rode into the forest, aiming north and west into the deepest regions of Wales. Summer had slipped away since he first came to the castle of Gornemant to be trained in arms, and during that time he had worked harder than he had thought possible. Even the old earl had been pleased with his progress. All the same, when Perceval decided to leave, Gornemant had objections. His training was incomplete, his shield arm needed another fortnight to heal, and autumn was wearing on, and would slip into winter early this year.

Perceval listened to the earl with the reverence due to an elder and benefactor, but the next morning at sunrise he was in the stable saying goodbye to his old pony Llech and saddling his war-horse Rufus. He rode away into the wilds with the sharp clean air of autumn scouring his lungs with every breath. As he looked into the colourless sky, he stretched away all the stiffness of the last months, and quickened his horse into a trot between his knees. He brought the animal to an easy canter and hummed a few bars of the *Gloria*. It was too long since he had slept under the cold stars.

He rode toward the mountains. Down in the grey-and-green valleys at their roots, the hush before wintry storms lay thick on the landscape.

Days passed. In the woods there had been settlements, farms, travellers, and the odd chance of a joust. Now he was alone, his silent musings set to the rhythm of his horse's hooves. His food, cold stiff hardtack, dwindled and vanished at last, and he fasted on black icy streams. Had there been anything else to eat, he would have killed and roasted it, but he seemed to have left every living creature behind.

Where was he going? At first he had intended to find some adventure, but very little had come his way before he wandered into this waste. Now, although he could always have turned back, something kept him pressing forward, some sense that this stillness and desolation signified something, if the interpretation could only be found.

And in the meanwhile, peace settled upon his soul. For the first time since his journey to Camelot, he had the luxury of solitude. Nothing came between him and the quiet voices of the world.

The land changed around him. Every day it became more

craggy and forbidding. Deep shadowed meres opened at his feet, sheer sunless sheets of rock barred his path, black clouds heavy with unshed snow loomed above him.

An evening came on stormy wings. The long twilight had begun at midday under frowning clouds that blocked the sun, but as the light began to fail altogether, a wind rose and began to clamour through the valley. Perceval hunched shivering into his armour. With a high-pitched whinny the wind flung the first snowflakes at him. He pulled on his helm for shelter, but the inside filmed over with water droplets at once.

Snow began to drift over the path, transmuting the landscape in bites and swallows from lead to silver. Perceval crested a low saddle, bending in the wind, looking in vain for shelter. Below and to the right, a desolate valley full of black stunted fir-trees ran away to the lowland. It looked kindlier than the mountainside, so he turned Rufus to pick his way down the slope.

Down in that valley the wind's bite blunted and the snow fell more gently. Perceval urged Rufus into a slow trot and followed the downhill course of a little black stream. Then the path took a sudden turn, and Perceval looked up and saw, in a cleft of the valley wall, a castle.

Like its surroundings, the castle was black and ruinous. All its outer walls had been shivered as if struck by lightning. Its gates lay in a twisted wreck, its battlements had fallen away like teeth in a battered mouth, and even the rooks' nests bristling from the walls seemed long deserted. The keep itself was seamed with cracks and the windows blind and black. Only one tower still remained standing, but in all its loneliness it was worth seeing, for a single light burned within it.

Perceval rode up into the keep, disturbing long-silent echoes.

Although the place was utterly shattered, he saw no weeds growing in the cracked pavement. He passed through a courtyard into the great hall where, to his astonishment, he found light and warmth. A fire was smouldering on the hearth, and torches lit the wall behind the high table.

He could not see a soul.

Perceval dismounted softly. Rufus bent and nosed the floor before discovering a bundle of provender in a corner. Perceval leaned his shield and lance against the wall, pulled off helm and gauntlets, and went warily to warm himself. There must be someone about, but were they friends or enemies?

As he held out his hands to the coals he saw a little table nearby set with red and white chess-pieces, ready for a game. Perceval brushed the dust off a stool and sat down, stretching his feet toward the fire.

Presently he picked up one of the chessmen to look at it. When he had blown and rubbed the dust away, he found that it was an ivory knight with shiny black eyes which seemed to return his scrutiny. He replaced it on its square and sat listening to the darkness and the shadows. After a moment, he rose and went to look out of the hall into the snowy courtyard.

Nothing. Nobody. He went back to the chess-table and sat down. Outside, the wind whispered along the roof-tiles. For a moment he imagined that the whole hall was full of shadowy presences, moving and talking under ghostly torches, but then he blinked, and was back in the desolate ruin. Perceval shook himself and moved the white queen's pawn forward two squares.

He was still looking at the board when a red knight slid forward in response.

Perceval sat up and stared into the darkness, hands stealing to the hilt of his sword.

Not a breath stirred the air.

Slowly Perceval reached out again and moved another pawn. Instantly the red king's pawn moved forward.

Perceval moved again, and the red responded almost before his fingers had left his own piece. Six moves later, he was checkmated. Perceval stared in bemused displeasure, and set the board again.

Twice more the red chessmen bested him, so easily that at the third defeat Perceval lost his temper entirely and rose to his feet, drawing his sword. "Come out, wherever you are!" he shouted.

"You are—you are—you are," the castle mocked.

Perceval passed his hand around the table, hoping to catch some thread used to move the pieces. There was none. He went to sweep the red pieces from the table, but they stuck firm.

Machine, or magic? The firelight had burned very low, and suddenly Perceval thought he heard footsteps far away. The hair prickled on the back of his neck and he swung his sword up meaning to smash the set and then take his chances with whatever was coming. But before he could move the castle broke its silence.

"No! Don't touch the chessboard," someone called. He was facing her before she had finished speaking. The first thing he saw was a white glimmer in the shadows behind the great table. Then she came closer and he saw her hair in the dark, a crown of sulky red which, being pinned to the top of her head, gave her the illusion of lofty height. It was the damsel in the pavilion, the damsel in the rain.

"Oh, it's you," she said, stopping short.

For the fraction of a moment, Perceval felt like a small

boy caught in mischief. Then in vexation he rebounded into something more than his usual nerve, shot his sword back into its sheath, and bowed with a flourish. "And still at your service, damsel."

"Oh, yes," she said with the same distant civility. "How is your arm, by the way?"

He had been unsure if she had seen his wound, and knowing that she had gave him a petty pleasure. "That? It was nothing, and is nearly mended. Tell me whom I have the honour of serving."

"My name is Blanchefleur, as they say here."

"I am Perceval, a knight of the Table," he told her, and the words alone lifted his chin and pulled his shoulders back. "And I crave your pardon for the wrong I did you in the pavilion."

Blanchefleur waved a cool and graceful hand, on which his mother's ring glinted. "You fought the Blue Boar for me. We are acquitted."

In her place, Perceval thought, he would have been angry, and this indifference perplexed him. "But I took your ring." He was wearing it on a thong around his neck these days, and pulled it over his head. "I am no robber of women. If it was given unwillingly, take it back."

She took it from him and stood doubtfully staring at the writing that ran around the inside of the band.

"What do the words say?"

Blanchefleur glanced up. "They speak of my mother." She held the ring out to him. "It was given willingly. Keep it."

He lifted his hand. "Not if it is precious to you."

"It isn't." The words were abrupt, and she paused. "I don't know my mother very well. Please take it."

Nothing loath, Perceval took the ring and grinned at her.

"And serve you also?"

"Serve me?"

He quoted his mother. "When a knight wishes to serve a lady, he will give her a ring from his hand and a—well, never mind that part. But of all ladies in the world, I would most gladly serve you, damsel, and repair the injury I did you."

"I have said that we are acquitted."

"No," he said.

She frowned. "No?"

"No," he said again. "I fought the Blue Boar for you, but I am a knight. I am bound to do as much for anyone, high or low, old or young, man or woman."

She tilted her head and looked at him with new respect. "What would you give me in recompense, then?"

"I would do as I offered. I would bear your ring and serve you a year and a day, taking no other lady during that space."

She gave him an odd look, with a twist like a smile at the corner of her mouth. "That is your request?"

"That? No. That I will do regardless. But if you would grant a request, you will wear my token during that time."

At that her eyebrow quirked up as if she meant to mock at him, but then the smile broke through and she was blushing and trying not to laugh and shaking her head all at once. Perceval wondered what it was that made her both so delighted, and so ashamed of being delighted. Almost every knight he had ever heard of had *some* lady to serve. What he suggested was no uncommon thing.

"I am silenced," she said ruefully, when at last she recovered her poise. "Have your wish, and come and eat."

The table on the dais was bare of anything but dust. When Perceval had wiped two of the weathered old chairs and a segment of the board, they took their seats at the empty table, facing the unfriendly mirk of the hall.

"Tell me how you come to be here in the wilds alone," he said, brushing his hands on his armour.

"Alone! Can you not see them? Not even a shadow?"

Perceval remembered the moment in which he had almost seen the hall lighted and full of people. "If they are here, I cannot see them."

"But you are from this world," Blanchefleur said, and they looked at each other with twinned confusion before she shook her head and went on. "I cannot see them either. But Naciens says they are all around us."

Perceval grinned. "One of them is very good at chess, then."

Blanchefleur laughed, and became serious again before he could return to the question he had first put to her. "Naciens said you have come here for a purpose."

Perceval thought of the long hushed days in the mountains, and nodded. "I thought so. Tell me what to do."

"You must take the message back to Camelot of what you have seen."

"What have I seen?"

"It's coming. Wait."

He leaned back into his chair, stretching out his legs. "As long as you want. That is, if there will be food."

"Naciens said there would be."

Silence settled back onto the castle. Perceval scanned the hall and finally fixed his eyes, like Blanchefleur, on the doors at the end of the room. The fire on the hearth had revived a little, but now it began to fade into a dull red glow. Even so, it was a lifetime before he knew he had not imagined the light stealing into the blackness beyond the door.

The doorway grew lighter by slow degrees. Then Perceval discerned singing voices, coming like the light from far away and moving closer. It was like nothing he had ever heard before, even in the old earl's chapel on Sundays, and he straightened in his chair to listen. The three voices sang simultaneously, but each wove a different melody in and around the others, so that the whole became a bewilderingly complex tapestry of sound. Yet the themes shared perfect clarity and perfect co-inherence. At no point did one voice overwhelm the others; at no point did they become confused.

It was like listening to the universe in motion. Planets spinning on their appointed courses, the lives of men intersecting and parting, the unimaginable harmony of the human body itself in hierarchy and order, were all implied in the song, but something greater as well: the genius of the composer, which must surely approach the miraculous. Perceval closed his eyes and was lost in the weaving music.

He came back to the waking world to find that the music had stopped. The light beyond the door still grew stronger, until he was sure that it would blind him if it shone any brighter. Then at last, with a triumphant blast of wind, its source appeared like the sun on a clear morning.

There were three veiled damsels. The first held a spear that dripped blood (its dark redness as positive and blinding as the white light)—blood that vanished before it could reach the ground. The second held a golden platter, and the third a cup covered with a thin veil. It was from the Cup that the light shone.

They paced up the hall. Perceval knew what he was seeing. His mother had told the story of Joseph of Arimathea, who gave his tomb for our Lord, coming to Britain in his old age with three incomparable treasures: the spear which had pierced Christ's side, the platter that had borne the bread at the Last Supper, and above all the cup from which he had drunk, with which Joseph had caught his blood running down the Cross. The cup of cups, the Holy Grail.

There was a rustle at his elbow as the Grail drew closer. Blanchefleur had pushed back her chair and sunk to her knees, blinking like an owlet in the light. Perceval moved with her. The damsels were passing them now. He could feel the light wash over them, almost tangible, and smell perfumes and spices for which he had no name, although they smelled like all the good memories of his childhood.

Then the Grail passed out of the hall, the light faded, and they were alone in the dark. Only a little light came from the fire. Perceval stood slowly, stiffly; groped for the dead torches on the wall and, finding them, coaxed them to life at the coals. In their rekindled light he saw Blanchefleur sitting in her chair again, a huddled and somehow smaller figure, staring unseeingly before her.

The table bore food, now—everything he most liked to eat, from fresh plums to milky cheese. But the sight of it could not distract him from what they had seen, and one thought sparked like fire in the dry tinder of his imagination, and leaped through him all at once.

"Now surely," he said, "the Quest of the Grail is close: the time they speak of, when the Grail Knight comes to Camelot and the knights of the Table ride out in search of the grace it holds."

Slowly, as if returning across vast distances of thought, Blanchefleur turned to him. "Yes. That was the message."

"It is close." Perceval drew a breath through clenched teeth.

"It is in my mind to go in search of it now."

"But the message—"

"They say it dwells in the castle of Carbonek—Carbonek, cut off from mortal lands. If the Grail is here, then Carbonek cannot be far away," and he was already striding down the hall to where he had left his arms and horse.

Blanchefleur pushed her chair back and came running down after him. "Perceval—" it was the first time she had used his name, and it sounded well, but he had no time to stop and listen to that music—"Perceval, you don't understand."

He pulled on his gloves and turned to her with his helm in his hands. "What? Do you know where it is? Is it near?"

She opened her mouth as if to speak, then caught herself, and shook her head. "You must go to Camelot first."

He pulled on his helm and fitted his shield to his arm. "Not before I have seen it again, just once."

"No! Wait and listen!" said Blanchefleur. But he swung into the saddle, laughing.

"I am coming back," he called. "I will bring you the Grail. Wait for me here."

"No, wait," she wailed again, but Perceval thrust the doors open and the wind swallowed her words. If she said anything else, it was lost in the clamouring echoes woken by his horse's hooves.

NOT UNTIL DAWN DID SIR PERCEVAL come fully to his senses. By then the snow had ceased, and the jubilant sun rose shining on dazzling whiteness striped by black trees. He sat looking at it in something close to despair. For the last hour he had believed that that glimmer on the horizon was the light he sought. When it finally broke above the trees he could no longer deceive himself.

Of course that castle was the Grail Castle. He had been in Carbonek herself. He had found the damsel of the pavilion again. He had seen the Grail, and he could have eaten from its provision. What had possessed him?

And what had he thrown away? Carbonek was cut off from the rest of Britain since Sir Balyn the Unlucky struck the Dolorous Stroke and maimed the Fisher King. No one found the road to Carbonek now, no one not watched over and guided by some gracious destiny.

Which he had flouted.

Was there still hope? He turned back to the west, and retraced his steps. For a few miles his trail was clear, but at last it vanished under last night's snow. The white-and-black of the forest held no clue. He pressed on while the sun rose higher, burning away the mist that lay in the valleys. Afternoon came, clear and bright. Then the day faded to evening and he knew he would not find Carbonek again.

Perceval reined in his horse and sat with bowed head, trying not to think how tired, hungry, and cold he was, or what a fool he had made of himself. Slowly the shadows grew deeper around him. More clouds were coming down from the North, piled up in gigantic purple and gold palaces, so that the sky looked like a window on Heaven.

Far above he heard a bird's scream, and looked up to see a hawk driving a dove across that sumptuous sky. The dove fluttered for the cover of trees, but the hawk folded its wings and dropped from higher air like a stone.

Perceval heard the soft *thud* of the two bodies meeting and saw crimson splash across the dove's breast. Three drops of blood chased each other down through the air and spattered on the snow, dark against dazzling white. Perceval stared at them and remembered Blanchefleur with her red hair and white tunic, the red stone of his mother's ring on her hand, and above all the drops of blood falling from the Spear at Carbonek.

While he sat musing, four knights came riding through the frosty air with a comfortable jingling of harness and with the breath steaming from their mouths as they talked and laughed. Sir Gawain was there with his cousin Sir Ywain, and Sir Kay, and King Arthur himself.

"Do you see that knight, sitting so listlessly staring at the snow?" said the King. "Do any of you know him?"

"His mount is familiar," said Sir Gawain, and chuckled. "He must be asleep, or witless, or deeply in love. He has not noticed us."

"Kay! Go and ask who he is," the King said.

"I'll stir him up, sire," said Sir Kay, and he came jogging up to Perceval and cried, "Sir! Ho, sir! Yonder is the Pendragon of Britain, and he wishes to know your name."

Perceval was aware of him, as if in a dream, and heard his voice, but not the words or the sense, and he did not lift his head or show any sign that he had understood. Sir Kay looked back to the King. "Hoy!" he suddenly shouted at Perceval.

Perceval, his eyes caught in the red and white and his mind in memory, still did not move, though he began to swim slowly to the surface of thought.

Kay waited a moment longer, and then lost his temper. "Answer me when I speak to you!" he said, and gave Perceval a clout on the head with his iron gauntlet.

Perceval came to himself then, boiling angry, reacting almost before he had a chance to think: swept up his spear-butt and with a satisfying *crack* returned the blow and laid Sir Kay senseless on the ground.

Then he looked up and saw the other three knights sitting there, watching. Laying his spear in rest he shouted, "Since it seems that nowadays a man must fight for a little peace and quiet, come on, all of you at once, if you wish!"

Gawain laughed, for he was fond of a bold speaker. "Sire," he said to the King, "surely that is the boy you sent on the adventure of the Queen's cup a while ago."

"Then go and give him my greetings," said King Arthur, "and perhaps now that he has beaten Sir Kay, he will let us pass in peace."

So Sir Gawain rode up to Perceval, his spear upright for peace, and said, "Sir knight, over there is the High King of Britain, who wishes to speak with you. As for this knight, this is Sir Kay, and he is not always as mannerly as he should be."

"I am glad to hear it is he," said Perceval, unhelming. "I warned him I would repay him the blow he gave to the maiden at Camelot."

"You charge a high interest," said Gawain, chuckling. He searched Perceval's face. "Your shield is blank, I see. What's your name and lineage, sir?"

"My name is Perceval, as I told you before," he said. "My mother's name was Ragnell and I do not know my father."

A look of delight danced in Gawain's eyes, and then he laughed, a long peal of pure joy, and turned back to King Arthur and Sir Ywain. "But I do, I think."

"Tell me!" Perceval urged, trotting his horse after. "Who was he?"

"My lord king," cried Gawain in the same delighted roar, "Here is my son, Sir Perceval."

Chapter 8

The Holy Grail!—
…
What is it?
The phantom of a cup that comes and goes?
Tennyson

WHEN THE ECHOES OF PERCEVAL'S GOING faded away, Blanche went back into the great hall of Carbonek and looked at the feast on the high table. More for something to do than because she felt particularly concerned about it, she divided the food into two parts and put half of it out in the passageway near the entrance, where it would be preserved by the autumn cold. Then she took her seat at the high table, but could not bring herself to eat. She was not hungry, and she did not want to eat in the cold and cavernous hall. She had seen it filled with light and music. She had sat at table with a companion more substantial than any of the whispering presences she half sensed in the shadows. Suddenly, and for the first time since she had come to Carbonek, she felt lonely.

She carried the rest of the food into her own little room, one of the few intact chambers in the castle. The room was dry and could be kept clean, but it was never completely warm or

83

light even with the fire burning and her candle lit. Naciens had given her few necessities and no comforts: plain food, a change of clothes, sleeping-furs, and a book. Then he had gone off with his mule on some urgent errand, and Nerys had returned to the house in Gloucestershire to meet Sir Ector and arrange their departure, and Blanche was left alone.

She had hardly noticed the solitude. She had been busy keeping house, or making camp, or whatever her life in this little room could be called. She had cooking, cleaning, and washing to do, and reading for when the time dragged. Above anything else, she had a firm and anchoring certainty that she was safe.

It had come to her on the night they had been hunted by Morgan, when Nerys sang on the hillside above Carbonek. It could not, of course, be compared to what she had felt a month or two back in her guardian's house, before she learned of Logres or Guinevere or the Queen of Gore, before she had known any cause of dread. Now she had escaped dogs and the sword, she might with justice have feared a whole host of shapeless threats, and yet the battlements of Carbonek surrounded her like the walls of a warm house in a winter storm. Perhaps that was what fended off the loneliness.

She was reading by the fire in her room one dark afternoon a week after she and Perceval had seen the Holy Grail when she heard the sound of hooves in the hall. Was it Naciens, wandering back from another pilgrimage, or some other stranger? Blanche wrapped herself in a cloak, went very softly down echoing black corridors to the hall, and peeked through the doorway. There was Naciens, sure enough. As he pushed back his hood, drops of water in his long white beard twinkled as though it really was made of snow. Beside him, speaking

84

quietly, there was a smaller, slighter figure holding a bay horse.

"Nerys!" Blanche called, and ran into the hall.

Nerys left off speaking to Naciens and turned with a smile to greet her.

"Are we leaving?" Blanche asked, as soon as courtesy allowed.

To her surprise, Nerys hesitated. She glanced at Naciens and said, "You understand that I can make no decisions on my own."

He bowed his head. Blanche looked from one to the other with curiosity.

"I thought you had come to take me to Camelot."

"I had," she said with a reassuring smile, and changed the subject.

They dined well from fresh store Naciens had brought in his saddlebags—a pair of moorhens and new brown flour which Blanche baked into cakes on the hearthstones in her room.

Nerys watched her with silent surprise. Blanche, glancing up, saw the look on her face and thought it better than any praise.

"Naciens showed me how to do this," she said.

"A month ago you couldn't even build a fire," Nerys said. "Now, you're cooking on one."

Blanche laughed. "It was rather dreary at first," she said. "But I learned to manage!"

She meant to ask what Nerys had been speaking to Naciens about, but was forestalled again. Dropping her voice almost to a whisper, Nerys said:

"Have you seen *it?*"

A week ago, Blanche might have been tempted to respond, "Seen what?" simply to assert herself as a free-thinker slow to believe extraordinary claims.

But she *had* seen it.

"Yes."

Nerys laughed, a little self-consciously, and tapped Blanche's cheek with her forefinger. "Yet you look no different."

"I am no different," the free-thinker wanted to say. Instead Blanche smiled and shook her head and gave the fowls another turn. Even if she had wanted to, she could not have put her experience into words, not yet.

Nerys's voice held years of longing. "Think of it, Blanche. The Holy Grail, here for the finding. Here for Logres. Naciens says the time is near."

"Yes."

"With the Grail,"—she was whispering now—"with the Grail, perhaps it can be done. A kingdom that shall never be destroyed…"

"Why, what are you talking about?"

Nerys quoted: *"Fiat voluntas tua, sicut in caelo et in terra."*

"But how?"

"How?" Nerys looked at her. "Didn't you feel it?"

"How can I know what I felt?"

"That I cannot tell you."

"But what did you expect?"

Nerys said: "They say that those who see the Grail are changed in will, so that they will in communion with the Divine will. Do you see now what it might mean for the Grail to come to Logres?"

Blanche stood up slowly from the fire, wiping her hands against the woollen skirt of her riding-habit. "No," she said at last. "I felt nothing of that kind."

Some of the light faded out of Nerys's eyes. Blanche, seeing it die, felt a twinge of conscience. What had Nerys suffered in the last eighteen years of exile? She had given up home and friends and loyalties, fled across the worlds, served as guard and governess. …And now the time came to return home to all those things she loved, and Blanche, the only reason for her exile, neither understood nor cared for them. No wonder that when Nerys fell prey to melancholy, the very stars seemed to weep.

Blanche spoke bitterly. "It should have been you, not me."

At that moment Naciens, having seen to the comfort of their beasts, came back into the room. Supper, although more satisfying than anything Blanche had eaten since the night of the Grail, could not overcome the sour taste left in her mouth from her conversation with Nerys. Yet what else could she have said? She had felt none of what Nerys described. And from the way Perceval had left Carbonek, it seemed plain that neither had he.

After supper, Naciens and Nerys left; no doubt, Blanche thought, to finish the conversation she had interrupted earlier. She was left to clean away the dinner things and brood. Nerys had returned to Britain. What would happen now? Would there be a chance to go back to the house in Gloucestershire, or was she trapped in Logres forever?

Blanche put another log on the fire and huddled into her furs, planning the best way to tackle Nerys. But when the elfin woman returned to the little warm room, her first words swept away every difficulty.

"We are going back to Gloucestershire in the morning," Nerys said.

Blanche blinked at her, then lit up in a smile. "You really mean it, Nerys?"

"Yes, of course." Nerys laughed.

A reprieve. Another chance. "Oh, thank you!"

"Only briefly, mind you. The rift between the worlds is

mended, but Logres is still the best place for you now. But you certainly cannot stay here in Carbonek—not like this." And she looked around the room with a shiver.

Blanche wondered what had happened to revive her spirits. As Nerys paced the room rubbing her hands and stamping her feet to work up some warmth, she seemed to shine like a lamp with happiness. But if there was a cause, she did not explain it, and at last she picked up the book Blanche had been reading that afternoon. "What's this?"

Blanche felt a little embarrassed to reply. After all, she was only reading it because Naciens had left her with nothing else. "The *City of God.*"

"Oh, yes. I read it eighty years ago. What do you think?"

"It's a good late example of Ciceronian rhetoric."

Nerys paused a moment, and again the light dimmed. "Yes, I suppose it is," she said, and after that, neither of them spoke until bedtime.

They left Carbonek early the next morning. Naciens rode his mule, and Blanchefleur perched on Florence's hindquarters behind Nerys. The snow which had fallen on the night Perceval came had long since melted and the starkness of the dead trees and shattered stones in the valley was unrelieved by snow or bud. Blanche, looking at the barren rocks from the castle gates, had felt that it was the most horrible place she had ever seen. But now she was struck not so much by the desolation as by the fact that the Grail dwelt here: so much light and richness in the unrelieved desert.

The sublime light and music came into her mind again. She understood, she thought, why Naciens should choose to live in this wilderness with the lost people of Carbonek—a people so very lost that they, and the relic they guarded, could not even be seen by visitors to the castle without a special grace. But then, she wondered, why the desolation, if the Grail was as marvellous as they said?

Naciens led them out of the trees, up a narrow path climbing the steep wall of the valley. In a little over an hour they dismounted in the place where they had first met him under the overhanging rock.

Whether it had been there all along, or whether the side of the hill had opened since last time, Blanche could not tell. But now there was a narrow cleft leading into darkness among the rocks.

Naciens said, "We are out of the Waste of Carbonek now. But I think, if you come this way again, you will find us."

Nerys held out her hand to Naciens. "Thanks, friend," she said. Then, to Blanche's discomfiture, she added, "Bless us before we go."

When this had been done, Nerys walked ahead of Blanche and Florence into the cleft in the hill. It became darker and darker as they went, until at last the blue thread of sky above vanished completely. The next moment they had all stepped out of the wardrobe in the hall of the house in Gloucestershire.

Nerys took Florence's reins and led her to the back door, now mended and replaced. When she opened it, Blanche saw that it was late evening, and the moon was shining.

She followed Nerys out onto the lawn. Here the air was mild, almost warm. The scent of roses and good rich earth rose around her. Somewhere in the orchard, a nightingale was singing.

Home, she thought, and drank in the air. But what brought them here? What had changed Nerys's mind?

Nerys was speaking to her, almost in a whisper. "Blanche,

find Sir Ector and tell him we've returned. Don't let the servants see you."

Blanche turned back to the house. The curtains in Sir Ector's study were drawn, but warm yellow gaslight streamed through the crack down the centre. Moving slowly, soaking in the mild air and delicious scents of autumn, she went to the French windows of the study and scratched on the door.

The curtain twitched aside. A moment later she had been caught into her guardian's bear-hug.

IN THE END IT TOOK SOME finessing before Blanche could call herself really at home. A charade had to be performed for the servants' sake: Nerys rang the front-door bell so that Sir Ector could pretend to have received a telegram, and the next morning he drove out in the barouche on time to meet the train and returned with Blanche and Nerys both dressed crisply and correctly, as though they had been on holiday at the seaside instead of roughing it in Britain.

But Blanche had slept in her own bed again, and woken late in the morning in warm and blissful content. She might soon be compelled to return to Logres, but at least they would never take her back to Carbonek!

Or *would* she return to Logres? Again, Blanche remembered Mr Corbin's words—"How can I help you if you speak of *musts?*" She had followed Nerys to Logres last time unthinkingly, reluctantly, frightened into submission by the Blue Boar's attack. She promised herself it would not happen again. Before she condemned herself to Logres for good, she would try, if she might, to find a way out. Perhaps Mr Corbin would be able to suggest something. She would go to the village to find him as soon as possible; this afternoon, maybe, or tomorrow.

Yet the thought of going to Logres did not seem so unbearable as it had before. Even Carbonek might have been worse. And there was the twinge of conscience she had felt when, for a moment, she had seen through Nerys's eyes. For a moment she had sensed what the fay had had to give up, and it had occurred to her for the first time that it was possible to love Logres, even to feel homesick for it...

And not only Nerys, but Sir Ector had made that sacrifice. For her. The least she could do was make an effort to understand their love, if she could.

Thus, when Sir Ector had fetched her home in state, and Blanche had looked over her correspondence and enjoyed an unhurried lunch, she went down to the library to find a book.

Her guardian was there, apparently dealing with some correspondence of his own. Blanche's heart sank at the sight of blue legal paper. So he was still preparing to close up the house and return to Logres. She had hoped that, whatever Naciens had told Nerys, it had postponed that at least for the next few months.

Sir Ector looked up at her with a smile. "Hullo, Blanche. Looking for anything?"

It occurred to her to look for something about Logres—wasn't there a famous book, *Le Morte D'Arthur* or something? But all her pride rose up in arms at the suggestion. She had given away her mother's ring, not once but twice, and she had quenched every spark of curiosity about her parents, and if she was bending now it was only for the sake of Nerys and Sir Ector, no one else.

Her conscience jabbed her. She pacified it with a moment's quick bargaining, and said to her guardian, "When I was at Carbonek I began reading *The City of God*. I'd like to finish it."

Sir Ector twiddled his pen. "In the English translation, or original Latin?"

"Latin, please," she said. Latin would undoubtedly make Nerys happier. And it left her conscience with no right to complain.

Sir Ector pointed. "Third shelf from the floor." But when Blanche found what she was after, she lingered.

"Are we going back to Logres soon?" she asked.

"Yes." Sir Ector laid down his pen. "But not right away. Nerys and I have much to arrange."

"Then is there time for me to see my friends before we leave?"

"Of course, Blanche. See them whenever you like."

"I was thinking of having a dinner party. I'd invite Kitty Walker, and Emmeline Felton. And Mr Corbin."

Sir Ector pushed his spectacles further up his nose and nodded. "I don't see why not. Arrange it whenever you like."

"Thanks," Blanche said. Still she didn't move. "And thanks for everything else, sir."

"Pardon?" He was already shuffling through the blue paper again.

"I know you must have been sorry to leave it all behind—Logres, I mean. Your home. You must have missed it dreadfully."

He looked up at her, blinked quickly two or three times and cleared his throat, and she knew he was deeply touched. "Yes. I do miss it."

"I don't love it like you do," she said, apologetically. "It seemed so cold and ugly."

"But you've only seen Carbonek!" said Sir Ector, with uncommon vehemence. "Nerys told me what a grim ruin it is now. But you should have seen it in the days before the Dolorous Stroke! The vale of Carbonek was full of song then!

All the apples in Logres went down that river to the sea. And you've never seen Camelot in summer. Camelot, the garden-city of Logres, full of towers and trees. You've never seen the sun on the windows of Carlisle, or walked in the river-side meadows of Trinovant in the spring."

"I suppose I haven't," Blanche said. It was hard not to get carried away on the tide of his enthusiasm. She said mournfully, "But you have friends there, too."

"The best brothers-at-arms a man could wish for. The most gracious King—" and something seemed to go wrong with Sir Ector's voice.

"Would I belong to anyone there?" Blanche asked.

Sir Ector blinked.

"Nerys told me there's some doubt. About me being the true heir of Logres. What about that? What will I have to face, there in Logres?"

Sir Ector looked out the window, playing with the coins in his pockets. At last he stood and walked around his desk to Blanche. "Prepare yourself," he said simply. "It's not going to be easy, Blanche. If you want your father's legacy, you'll have to fight for it."

Blanche kept her eyes on the carpet. "What if he isn't my father?"

"If he doesn't doubt it, why should you?" Sir Ector raised her chin with one finger and kissed her on the forehead. "I raised him, Blanche, and I can tell you this as surely as if it came from his own lips: he won't desert you."

That was exactly what she was afraid of. She didn't say it out loud. "How much time do I have left at home?"

"It depends," he said, becoming more vague and more businesslike, all at once. "As a matter of fact, Nerys and I will need to go to Camelot to speak to the King before we know."

"To make sure that he really does want me?" she asked, just to be contrary.

"No, no, no, Blanche!" Sir Ector sighed. "When Nerys went to Carbonek to fetch you, Naciens the Hermit told her something which upset all our plans. He says they need you at Carbonek."

Carbonek. Ugly, funereal, holy Carbonek. *What?*

"Do you know what the Grail Maiden is?"

"I don't."

"The maiden guardian of the Holy Grail. She watches, and prays, and contends. Since the fall of Elaine, eighteen years ago, there has been no Grail Maiden. Naciens says that you have been chosen for the next."

Chapter 9

And when he came to the Tearne Wadling,
The baron there co'ld he finde,
With a great weapon on his backe,
Standing stiffe and stronge.
The Marriage of Sir Gawain

"I SAW THE LADY OF THE Lake last night, riding north," said the King.

They were camping on the hills of Powys, roasting venison and their faces over a campfire built high and blazing to fend off the nip of frost at their backs. For once the clouds had withdrawn, unveiling the bitter stars and ice-haloed moon.

Perceval had been remembering his first journey to Carbonek, and how hushed and lonely it was by contrast to this good fellowship. Then the King's words fell into a momentary silence, and they all stirred and took interest.

"A dream?" Sir Ywain asked.

"No, it was herself. She said she would meet me in Camelot by All Saints."

"To what purpose?" There was a combative gleam in Sir Kay's eye.

The King sighed, as if picking up the thread of an argument

long standing. "She has always shown us friendship, Kay."

"She is a fay," Kay reasoned. "She may not mean us harm, but she will do it sooner or later."

Sir Gawain, whetting his sword, looked up. "We know the Lady Nimue can be trusted."

"Why are you defending her? You know better than any of us what harm comes when Elves meddle with men, however good their intentions."

Silence fell, as breathless as the space between lightning and thunder. Perceval saw the others slowly straightening to look at his father.

No thunder came. Instead Gawain said quietly, "Yes. I know it."

A pause. Ywain said, "Harm, Gawain? I should never have expected to hear *you* say so."

"Everything comes with a price."

"Then the price of an immortal love is too high for me," laughed Kay. "How long did you wander around Camelot looking like Saint Sebastian's ghost?"

At that they all laughed. But Gawain reached out to grasp Perceval's shoulder. "I meant something else. I did not even know I had a son until yesterday. I had both paid and profited more than I knew."

"What does that have to do with the fay?" Perceval asked, curious.

Gawain stared. "Did you not know? Your mother was one of Nimue's people."

Perceval searched his father's face, unsure whether he was joking. "A fay? Mother?" He glanced around the fire. Not even Sir Kay was laughing up his sleeve. "She never told me…"

"Never?"

Perceval shook his head. "I wonder why."

"Perhaps she was afraid you'd follow her." Gawain put his hand over his mouth; there were tears in his eyes. "She could have taken you, you know. To the west, to Avalon. You could have become one of them. Ageless. …Instead, she sent you to me."

Perceval grinned. "What, me go to Avalon? No fear of that. I wanted to be up and doing, sir father."

Gawain blinked, and smiled back at him. "Yes. You would think so. But it was no small sacrifice for your mother."

Perceval tried to imagine what it might be like to turn his back on the splendid war of the world and retreat to Avalon, the peaceable isle. He laughed at the thought and said, "But this explains why everyone feared her and called her a fay. Why did she leave you, if she loved you?"

"The price of marriage to a mortal. The laws of her people took her from me after seven years. Did you really never hear the story?"

"Never."

A faint smile crossed his face. "She left that for me, too. Well, she was one of the people of the Lake, and my aunt, the sorceress, loved her brother."

Perceval glanced at the King and Sir Ywain. "Morgan le Fay? Is she an Elf, too, then?"

Sir Ywain stirred. "My mother," he said slowly, for he was always reluctant to speak of her, "is no fay, although she calls herself that. She was the daughter of the Queen Igerne and her first husband, the Duke of Tintagel. Full sister to Morgawse, the Queen of Orkney, your grandmother. Half sister to the King. There is not a drop of real fay's blood in her veins. Go on, cousin."

Gawain said: "When Ragnell and her brother refused to sell Morgan the secrets of their people, she enchanted them both. The brother, Sir Gromer Somer Joure, she bound to her evil will in the fortress of Tarn Watheline. But Ragnell, Ragnell she changed into the loathliest creature you could imagine if your eyes had drunk their fill of Hell itself."

Perceval's scalp prickled. "Morgan was able to do all this? Christ guard us all."

"He does. But Ragnell and her brother were unbaptised then. For the Elves say they are beyond salvation." He turned to the King. "The next part is your story, sire."

Arthur smiled. "An inglorious one, I have always thought, compared to yours."

"I have known the King of Logres since we were boys together, and he has done nothing inglorious in all that time," said Gawain, inclining his head.

"No? But if I have done anything worthy of praise, it is only that I have gathered praiseworthy men around me."

"Only a mean man seeks the company of mean men, sire."

"You honour me, fair nephew. But today I claim no more than my right, which is to win the honour of honouring one who merits it. I will tell the tale."

That was a game they played between them, these warriors of the Table—if it could be called a game, when done with such sincere gravity. The name of it was courtesy. Perceval listened, but he did not yet dare to play it with them.

The King went on. "At Christmas that year I held court at Carlisle. When a maiden came and sought justice for the tyrant of Tarn Watheline, I determined to undertake the quest myself.

"Not until I rode onto the bridge of Tarn Watheline to challenge Sir Gromer Somer Joure did I discover that the damsel had betrayed me to my death. For she was one of my sister's maidens. When my horse's hooves struck the bridge, all my power left me, so that I could hardly sit upright in the saddle. Then I looked up, and saw the lord of Tarn Watheline standing there, and he was a tall man, so that mounted as I was, our eyes were on a level."

"And I have always said that he grows taller each time you tell the tale, sire," said Sir Kay.

"That is why I keep you with me, good Kay," said the King without anger. "Nevertheless, as I sat upon the bridge of Tarn Watheline, I could not lift a finger, and I knew that I would be but a dead dog if I could not rescue myself. 'Think on your sins, O King,' he said.

" 'Think on your own,' I said. 'For your last days have come, and although I am at your mercy now, my justice shall certainly find you after my death. A hundred of the best knights of Logres sit feasting in Carlisle, and they know where I have gone and on what errand. If I do not return, they know my will.'

"That puzzled him. Then he said, 'A bargain.'

" 'Say on,' I said, for I was not so sure of myself as I seemed.

" 'I will give you a year and a day,' said the knight of Tarn Watheline. 'Answer this question: what is it that women desire above all things? If you can answer me this in a year and a day, you shall go free. But if you cannot answer, I will have your head, and the knights of Logres shall leave me in peace.'

" 'It is a bargain,' I said. And then the weakness left me, and I rode back to Carlisle alone, for my sister's damsel had stayed only long enough to jeer at me."

The King turned to Sir Gawain. "Now you shall tell the rest of it, Gawain, for it is your story."

Gawain nodded. "When the King told me of the bargain he had made to save his life, the task did not seem difficult. But at the end of a year and a day, when he and I had ridden the length and breadth of Britain, we had a thousand different answers from a thousand different women. Some wanted wealth, some wanted idleness, some wanted richer homes or nobler husbands. And we both knew that the true answer must be something else entirely. We were within a league of Tarn Watheline when we met *her*."

"She was foul beyond description," interjected Sir Kay. "One eye beneath her snout, and the other in the midst of her forehead. All clothed in scarlet, with yellow tusks gleaming in the last light of sunset. I saw her at the wedding."

Perceval shuddered. "This was Mother?"

"You should have seen *mine*, on the night of the new moon," said Sir Ywain, eyes gleaming with unwonted laughter. "Go on, cousin."

"The loathly lady asked us our business, and although we felt that nothing could save Logres now, not even one more answer, we spoke her fair.

" 'I know this baron,' said the lady. 'And I know this riddle, and will tell you—for a price.'

" 'If it is one that may be paid with honour,' said our good King.

" 'That is for you to determine,' said the loathly lady. 'I wish to wed one of your knights, lord King.' Do you remember, sire?"

"I remember it well," said the King, poking the fire.

"So do I," Gawain said. "I remember a time of silence, and then I remember how slowly you turned your head and looked at me with a manner that seemed to say, 'Why, here's Gawain, a bachelor.' "

100

"And then I told you that if you loved me, you would not burden my conscience with such a sacrifice."

"I did not do it for you, sire." Gawain was deadly serious now. "Death comes to us and all mortals. I shall still lose you one day. But Logres! The only perfection under heaven would fall if I could not save you."

"Not perfection, Gawain. Not Logres. Not yet."

Perceval's father smiled. "Well. The loathly lady told us the answer to the riddle. When we came to Tarn Watheline, Sir Gromer Somer Joure was waiting for us. And we read all the answers we had gathered.

" 'All so much warm air,' said the knight. And he heaved up his mace.

"And the King said, 'Wait! As we came, we met a loathly lady all clad in scarlet, and she told us that the thing women desire above all other things is *their own will*.' "

("It is true," said Sir Kay. "And not only for women," said the King.)

"The knight of Tarn Watheline fell into a rage. 'It was my sister Ragnell who revealed this to you,' he said, but although he gnashed his teeth and called down curses upon her head, there was nothing he could do.

"So the King repaid his vow and was free, and I gained a wife. We married in the view of all at Carlisle, and there was no dancing and little piping at our wedding. Not even the children in the street had the heart for it. But when the sun went down and we were alone, she returned to her true form. And her beauty after the horror was like all the fires of heaven."

He spoke slowly, here, as if by drawing out the telling of it he could draw out the memory. "I thought I was dreaming. Or mad.

"But she said to me, 'You have broken half the curse. But I shall be fair only half the time. Choose whether I shall be fair by day, or fair by night.'

"I said, 'By day I must travail and fight, from one end of Britain to the other. Be fair by night, when I am there to see you.'

" 'But think!' she said. 'By day I must sit in bower, and brave the pity and horror of everyone who sees me. At least, at night, the darkness will cover me.'

"Then I yielded my desire to her choice. But she replied: 'There will be no choice. For those words have broken the spell entirely.'

"And we had seven years."

CLEAR NIGHT GAVE WAY TO CLEAR morning. The water in their bottles had frozen, and not until the sun rose high enough to touch it did the frost vanish from the grass. Sir Perceval, following his four companions in single file down the slope of a hill, closed his eyes, leaned back, and basked in warm sun. Then Rufus stopped and he opened his eyes to see that the others had reined in and were speaking.

"I have passed this way before, sire," Sir Ywain was saying, pointing to the towers of a castle rising through trees in the valley below. "This is the castle of Sir Breunis."

"I have heard of him," Sir Gawain said. "A robber of women and old men. It is his custom to stop travellers and demand ransom."

"Let us turn aside here, then," said the King.

The castle of Sir Breunis was a small keep in a green valley amidst unkempt farmland. Some scores of paces from the gate his shield hung from an oak-tree. Sir Gawain spotted it at once.

"Watch this," he said to Perceval. He trotted up to the shield, and dealt it a ringing blow with the butt-end of his spear.

"Gawain!" Sir Ywain protested over the echoes. "This man rifled my father's steward three months ago. I had sworn to myself the right of retribution."

"Wait, gentlemen," said the King. "We have an untried knight with us. Of your courtesy, let him fight."

Perceval looked his gratitude. But his spirit cooled when he glanced up at the sound of hooves and saw a gigantic knight emerging from the castle bearing the same sable shield that hung on the oak-tree. His voice boomed inside the helm.

"Well, well—I see the lion of Ywain, the pentacle of Gawain, and the dragon of Uther's son. Has Camelot emptied to fight me?"

"No," Perceval shouted back. "They have come to watch."

He felt rather than saw the four others move to the wayside, off the path, which seemed even lonelier without them at his back. But it was too late to complain. The enemy was already moving. He laid his spear in the fewter, breathed, "Jesu, defend me!" and clapped his spurs to Rufus's sides. The great horse gathered himself and leaped forward like a thunderbolt. Perceval's eyes narrowed on his target. He measured out fractions of seconds with crystal clarity and was conscious, despite the speed at which his enemy surged closer, that his own form was perfect and he could not fail to strike true.

With a bone-wrenching shock they met. The spear in Perceval's hand melted away into wooden shards. Rufus reeled and staggered. The landscape spun wildly and then the road reared up and slammed against him.

The double shock and the taste of dust were familiar enough from his training at the old earl's castle: he had been unhorsed.

Perceval gritted his teeth, rolled, and staggered to his feet, drawing his sword. Through the slit of his helm he saw his four companions standing under the oak tree. Then Rufus, moving off the road in a daze. Perceval whirled, searching for his enemy. As he did so, something blocked the sunlight and he threw up his shield just in time to catch Sir Breunis's sword. Not until he had evaded the blow and retreated a step or two did he have the time to realise that the other knight, too, must have been unhorsed. Also he was wounded, with the blood already running down his sword-arm.

The sight flooded through Perceval's veins like new life, and sluiced away the shock, not to mention the embarrassment, of his fall. The combat had hardly begun, but victory was already within his grasp. He yelled, and rushed Sir Breunis with a storm of blows. The enemy guarded himself, but his wound made him sluggish, and he staggered back under Perceval's assault. Then he rallied, and Perceval felt some of that gigantic strength.

He danced back a few steps, hoping to weary the enemy knight by forcing him to follow. But Sir Breunis knew better than to waste his strength, and took the opportunity to breathe. Perceval rushed in again, lunging for the right shoulder, left unprotected by a drooping shield arm. What came next happened so fast that his eyes could barely follow: Sir Breunis parried his lunge with such a powerful stroke that Perceval spun under the impact, turning his unshielded right flank towards the enemy. At the same moment, Sir Breunis snatched a poniard with his left hand and aimed it for the underarm joint of Perceval's armour.

All this Perceval saw and understood in a fraction of time. The only question was whether he was too overextended to take the quick step back that would save him...no. He recovered and disengaged. The glittering blade no more than kissed his mail. All the enemy's attention was on the poniard, leaving his sluggish sword-arm still out of play through that flailing parry; he left himself, for a moment too long, unguarded. …Perceval laughed and lunged, every ounce of bone and muscle flung behind his sword's point, and thrust with tremendous force clean through his foe.

They stood face to face, panting through the bars of their helms. Sir Breunis lifted the poniard in his left hand and drove it at Perceval's extended arm. It was a futile gesture: the mail at that point, unlike the clumsy ring-stitched leather the brigand wore, was too fine-woven for the blade to find entrance. Perceval recovered his lunge. Sir Breunis staggered back off the blade and fell to the ground, clutching his wound.

Perceval stood, rasping in great breaths of air. Dimly he was aware of his father and the King coming toward him. Then he remembered what came next, drew his own poniard, and cut the laces of Sir Breunis's helm.

The bandit's face twisted with agony underneath his big black beard. Perceval held the poniard to his throat with trembling hands.

"Do you yield?" he asked.

Protests reached Perceval's humming ears, it seemed, from far away. "No! Kill him!" Sir Kay was saying.

"I yield, I yield," gasped Sir Breunis.

"If you let him live, more innocent travellers will suffer," said Sir Ywain.

Perceval looked down at the man's vice-ravaged face and shuddered. Sir Gawain was saying, "Better put an end to him, boy. Let justice be done."

The word reminded Perceval of the King. "Sire?" he croaked.

Arthur stepped over the wounded man and knelt on the other side, removing his helm. He glanced up at Perceval and said, too quietly for the others to hear, "Well done." Then he looked down at Sir Breunis.

"Do you wish to live?"

A nod.

"You know who I am," said the King. "Say my name."

Breunis grimaced and groaned and got it out. "Arthur Pendragon. High King."

"Then you know what charge is upon me. You have robbed and pillaged my people. You have robbed and pillaged *me*. If I do not avenge them, who will?"

The man was silent.

"Answer me. Tell me why I should spare you."

"They say that no one ever asked your mercy in vain…"

That was bold, perhaps bolder than Perceval himself would have been in such a case, and he half expected the King's anger to kindle.

But Arthur Pendragon nodded. "It is true. And it does not delight me to kill and maim, but neither do I give my mercy freely. The cost is your freedom. You must become my man. You must swear to abandon your pillage, restore their property to those you have robbed, and put your strength at the service of all oppressed ones, wherever you may meet them, for as long as your life is spared upon the earth. Will you so swear?"

"I swear it." The brigand began to sob, loud heaving cries. "I swear it. Let me live, O King."

Perceval, sickened by that abject plea for mercy, suddenly despised him, and the hand holding the poniard went ice-steady. But the King said:

"I give you your life, then, sir, what's left of it. See that you mend yourself and abandon this habitual thievery, for if I hear otherwise you will surely die."

He nodded to Perceval, who with a mixture of relief and disappointment shot his poniard back into the sheath and picked up his bloody sword. The King rose and turned to his knights.

"Sire," said Gawain with a note of reproach in his voice, "your mercy is too sublime for my understanding. This man is worthy of death."

"So too are we," said the King. "Have the castle thrown open and thoroughly searched."

Kay and Ywain went up the road to see to this, but Gawain held his ground. "We? How so? We are your majesty's instruments of justice. And your majesty's justice is the justice of Heaven."

"Fair nephew," said the King, "all this is true, I hope, especially that I am ruled by the justice of Heaven. And yet, Gawain, we are sinful men."

Perceval flopped to the ground and watched the King and Sir Gawain with a furrowed brow, wiping his sword on the grass by the wayside.

Gawain was saying, "We are sinful men, sire, but this man is beyond saving."

The King laughed. "God help me, Gawain, if you were ever to read the sin in my soul."

"I know you better than to think it might be found there, sire," said Gawain, with an oddly sweet smile lighting up his harsh face.

But the King's laughter had faded. He glanced at Sir Breunis, whose men had come from the castle to carry him in.

"Do not deceive yourself, Gawain. There are black places in

the heart of every man."

Perceval thought of the disappointment he had felt when the King gave Sir Breunis his life, and was suddenly ashamed. As Sir Breunis's men lifted him onto a handcart, Perceval ran to him.

"You have taken as your lord the best man of the world," he said, gripping the sides of the cart on each side of the wounded knight's head. "You know it."

At first Breunis threw back his stare from a blank face. But then he dropped his gaze and grunted: "I know it."

"That makes us brothers." Perceval spoke slowly to let each word, with its weight of menace, sink in. "But if I find that you have deceived him, you will die by my hand. I swear it."

Chapter 10

Then they showed him the shield, of shining gules
With the pentangle pictured in pure gold hues.
Sir Gawain and the Green Knight

ONE WET EVENING IN LATE OCTOBER the five knights-errant rode out of the forest and saw the grey bulk of Camelot rising gently from its little green hill under low dark clouds and plashing rain. Light shone from a hundred windows and glimmered off the deep swift river-water at the hill's foot. Over the bridge they rode, up into the town, with doors slamming open and voices calling news and welcomes. The King pulled off his helm so that he could be seen, acknowledging the news and returning the greetings.

They had ridden hard all day to be back at sundown, and when they reached the castle courtyard Perceval was glad to slide from his saddle, hand the reins to a squire, and walk stiffly after the others into the keep. Here they were met by a flock of maidens. Two of them took Perceval by either hand and led him away without a word. He glanced back at the others, almost in a panic, and saw them being spirited off likewise. From the door into the Great Hall he heard the buzz of voices, saw the warm blaze of candles, and smelled meats and spices that made his stomach growl—but it was already too late to say anything, for he had been swept into a dark passage, and could only blindly follow his maiden guides.

They brought him to a room on the east side of the castle, not large but by far the most luxurious place he had yet seen, with clean rushes underfoot and thick bright tapestries to shut in the warmth. These were worked with trees and grotesquely beautiful creatures he did not recognise, so that for a moment he thought he stood in some foreign and oppressive wood. The hearth was wisely built, drawing the smoke off the fire and filling the room with heat. Perceval, accustomed to the crisp free air and endless halls of the forest, stood still in dumb amazement while the two maidens whisked off his armour. A third brought him a cup of heated and spiced wine, and then hot water and a flannel.

When they ushered him back to the Great Hall, Perceval hardly knew himself—clean and warm, clad in soft new wool under the fur-lined robe worn by knights in time of peace. Although they were inexpressible ease to his weary body, something about the warm furs, the scented heat of the fire, and the all-embracing tapestries had disquieted him, and when the maidens bore away his armour for cleaning and repairs, he had almost begged them to leave him his sword—then felt a little foolish when they silently returned it to him, and found a new belt, not clogged with mud and rain, for him to hang it from.

But with the heft of it at his hip he felt more of a man, and less of a house-cat, and better able to walk into the Great Hall, and the company of the knights of Logres.

He could not help remembering the last time he had been here, at the Feast of the Ascension with the hall in an uproar over the insult he had avenged. But here was a peaceful, almost a domestic scene: the Queen at the head of the Table plying the King with food, a hum of conversation from the ladies in the balcony, a louder chatter from the long tables where the squires and servants sat, and little knots of knights clustered among the empty spaces at the Round Table, deep in talk.

Perceval paused, uncertain, in the doorway—did he belong at the Table, or with the squires and wanderers? But then a foot fell on the rushes behind him and he turned to see Sir Gawain, who beckoned him to the Table.

"Gawain! About time!" said one of the knights, rising from his seat, and Perceval blinked at him, for the smile which flashed across his face seemed a duplicate of Gawain's. "Who have you brought with you?"

Gawain seemed to expand slightly. "Cast your eyes over the Table, lads, and see if there's a place for Sir Perceval...*mab* Gawain."

"What's that?" someone asked, and Perceval found himself surrounded by a curious ring of onlookers.

"Sir Perceval's seat is over by the Siege Perilous; the letters appeared at midday," said the knight who had spoken first. "What do you mean, *mab* Gawain? I've a grown nephew? Why was I not told?"

"I could not have known, myself," said Gawain. "Ragnell left without telling me."

"I thought she had gone to Avalon."

"Not until last spring."

"And you say you knew nothing about it?"

"Sir Gareth, we do not starve information out of our captives here." It was a lady's voice, cool and imperious. But when Perceval glanced at the Queen, he saw that she was laughing.

111

Sir Gawain laughed with her, and said to Perceval, "This is my brother, Gareth. Now come and eat. No, no, Caradoc, later. Gaheris, I'll see my new niece after I eat, or I may eat her. Perceval. Your siege."

Like all the others it was a big, square-hewn wooden chair, carved with leaves and acorns, and bearing letters on the back in gold: *Sir Perceval of Wales*. Gawain's own siege was next to him on the right. On the left was an empty seat with no words on it at all.

"What's this?" he asked, but Gawain was piling food onto his trencher and did not hear.

"This? This is the Siege Perilous. Never sit in it, as you value your life." Sir Gareth kicked away the seat on the other side of the Siege Perilous (it was labelled *Sir Bors*) and sat on the Table.

Perceval nodded, and leaned back for the serving-man to give him bread and a partridge. "I've heard of it. It is intended for the Grail Knight?"

"Yes. Anyone else who sits there—*fzzt*, he turns to flame and ash."

Perceval remembered the damsel Blanchefleur's message, which he had given to the King in the hills of Wales. "He will come soon."

Gareth nodded. "The King told us. When will it be?"

"I know nothing more, neither the day nor the hour." Perceval paused before biting into the meat. "It is strange to find an uncle. Are there more?"

"Two more," Gareth told him. "Gaheris is over there." He pointed. "Agravain is gone on some quest or another."

Perceval swallowed. "And your father?"

"King Lot of Orkney, dead many years. Mother—Queen Morgawse—rules now. Then there are the cousins. Ywain you know. He's the son of Uriens King of Gore."

"And of the Queen of Gore."

Gareth laughed softly. "Our sweet aunt Morgan. Yes. But Ywain is like his father. Mordred is like—Mordred is *not* like his father."

Gawain turned to them.

"Mordred," he said, frowning. "Have you seen him, brother?"

"Not for months." Gareth squinted across the Table and sighed with mock disappointment. "He must be alive somewhere. His siege still bears his name."

"Gareth!" said Gawain, but his reproachful voice shook with laughter. "What has he done to deserve that?"

"Nothing," returned Gareth. "Ah, Gawain, you are right. Mistrust is an ugly guest, and the only one not welcome among brothers." He turned to Perceval again. "Gaheris and I are married men, and can give you cousins of your own, but they are yet young to break spears."

Perceval was beginning to speak, but when the other knights fell silent and Sir Gareth slipped off the Table, he turned to see what had made them all stand up so straight.

It was the Queen. The back of his mind noticed that he, too, had stiffened as if to attention. Perceval had lived with the immortal beauty of his mother all his life, but even he was awed by Guinevere.

She set a silver and glass cup before him. "You sent this back and avenged the slight upon me," she told him. "The cup is yours now."

"I thank you, madam."

She smiled, and walked on. "Goodnight," she said in a louder voice. "Sleep well, and sleep safe. Ye are guards on the borders of darkness: look upon what you protect, and rest from your

113

labours. Goodnight!" And she passed from the hall.

AS NOVEMBER BLEW IN, TURNING THE forest to grey smoke, Perceval stayed at Camelot, for here he had the chance to continue his training under the eye of his father and other knights of the Table.

There was also an item of business that had to be finished before he could undertake another quest. Sir Gawain took him one afternoon to see Sir Bleoberis, the King's herald, about a device of his own.

The knight was surprised to hear that Perceval had been using a blank shield. "Surely," he said, reaching down a folio stuffed with painted parchments, "you used *something* to signify your name and lineage."

"I had not the slightest idea of my name and lineage, sir," Perceval said cheerfully.

"Well. Look at these." Sir Bleoberis produced a parchment showing a white shield bearing red diagonals. "*Argent*, three bendlets *gules*. You know this one, of course."

Perceval squinted thoughtfully. "Oh, that is Sir Lancelot's shield."

"Right. And here—*Argent*, a dragon passant *gules*."

That was more familiar—the King's own shield, with its red dragon. "The Pendragon. What about Father? A red shield with a yellow star."

"Here it is," said Sir Bleoberis. "*Gules*, a pentacle *or*. But the question remains what bearings you should carry. I meant to show you this." He extracted a sheaf of parchments and spread them out.

Gawain leaned over to look. "Here are the Orkney arms." He pointed to a purple shield bearing a double-headed golden eagle. "Gareth, Gaheris, and Agravain bear variations of this."

"Why do you have something different?" Perceval asked.

From the look that fleeted across Sir Bleoberis's face, Perceval wondered if he had said something wrong. But Gawain bent his head and traced the pentacle with his forefinger, answering without heat. "The Endless Knot signifies the five virtues of knighthood. And these are generosity, fellowship, purity, courtesy, and compassion. I took it to remind me of them."

"Then there is nothing I had rather bear," said Perceval.

Sir Bleoberis picked up the parchment and pursed his lips. "We should have to differ it from your father's shield, to prevent confusion."

"Label it," Gawain said. "When I am dead, he can remove the label."

Sir Bleoberis took a new parchment and dipped his pen in ink. "*Gules*, a pentacle *or*, bearing a label of three points *or*. I will enter it in the rolls."

ON AN EVENING NOT LONG AFTER this, Perceval was on his way to Sir Gareth's rooms when Sir Kay passed him in the passage with a woman shrouded in a black cloak, glistening with rain. He caught a gleam of eyes from within the hood, and then the lady put her hand on Sir Kay's arm to stop him.

"Sir Perceval," she said. "Come with us to the King's solar."

Perceval wondered how she knew him and looked at Sir Kay half-expecting a reaction. But even Sir Kay dared not gainsay this lady. "If you think so, madam."

"I am sure of it," she said, and passed on.

Perceval waited only to send a page with a message to Sir Gareth, then followed Sir Kay and the stranger to the solar. This was a warm room on the south side of the castle, welltapestried against the cold, where in his few leisure hours the King could often be found playing chess or hearing the news of knights-errant. He sat there now with the Queen by him and an assemblage of the older knights: Sir Gawain, Sir Lucan, Sir Bedivere, Sir Ywain, and Sir Kay.

In other words, a gathering of the King's council. Perceval bowed deep, wondering what he might have done to draw their attention. But then the lady he had met in the Great Hall turned from the fire, where she had been warming herself, and came to him with an outstretched hand.

"Sir Perceval," she said, "do you know me?"

She had laid aside her cloak and wore a robe sheened with silver threads like water. Her hair, tied into a long black braid, snaked almost to the floor. Her face—but when he looked at her face, he wanted to fall to his knees and grip the ground to know that it was still there, that he was not suddenly floating lost and anchorless in vast starry spheres.

With an effort he stiffened his knees and remembered when he had last sensed that overpowering immensity. This woman was a fay.

"The Lady of the Lake."

She smiled, and the stress of her regard lessened a degree. "Very good."

Gawain said: "Now that he is here, let us begin. You have yet to explain what he has to do with the King's daughter."

"A little, son of Lot. And more hereafter, if I see clearly. He has spoken of the errand given him at Carbonek Castle?"

"That the Grail Knight draws near? He has," said the King.

"And, sir knight,"—to Perceval—"do you remember the name of the damsel who gave you this message?"

"She said her name was Blanchefleur." His mouth went dry

116

all of a sudden, and he gulped. "The King's daughter?"

No one heard his question. The King was speaking to the Lady of the Lake. "She is here, in Britain?"

"She was in Carbonek, and has returned to the other world now," said Nimue. "But I have seen her keepers and they say they must speak to us, Lord Arthur. She is no longer safe in hiding. Morgan has already been there."

"Then it is time for her to come home," said the King. "We have been too long without her company."

A slight frown wrinkled the Queen's brow.

"Remember the reason you sent her away," said Nimue.

"That she might be safe until the time comes to fulfil the prophecy," said the King. "Yes. But if Morgan has found her way to the other place, she will be safer here."

"Even Camelot has not always protected you, O King," Sir Ywain put in. "My mother has the cunning of a rat in a garderobe."

"And yet I am still alive," the King said.

"You face the danger for Logres's sake, sire," said the Queen, speaking for the first time. "But Blanchefleur is yet young for such burdens."

"Is she?" The King spoke gently, to make the words less harsh. "She can be no younger than Sir Perceval, here, whom I have seen adventure his life in combat. One day she must carry Logres. I only hope we have not kept her unburdened too long."

"There is another choice, besides Camelot," said the Lady of the Lake. "With safety, but also hardship, and a certain kind of danger."

The others in the room looked at her in surprise. "Say on," said Arthur.

Nimue said: "I was riding in the night through Torfaen when I met the Hermit of Carbonek, waiting for me at the Greyflood crossing. 'Tell the High King,' he said, 'that Sarras needs a maiden.' "

"Sarras!" Arthur put up a hand to smooth his beard over his chin. "And his meaning?"

"The maiden guardian of the Holy Grail," said Nimue. "They want Blanchefleur at Carbonek."

"Have you been there, lady? To Carbonek?"

"No." There was a hint of wistfulness in her voice. "The damsel Nerys has been."

"She and Sir Ector are right, then. I must speak to them. But who will guard Blanchefleur while they travel?"

Nimue said, "Send a knight you trust. Sir Perceval here has already fought Sir Odiar of Gore on her behalf."

"What?" Perceval, jerked so suddenly into the discussion, spoke without thinking. "Not me, I beg you."

"Why not?" asked Sir Gawain with knitted brows.

Perceval turned to the King. "Sire, I will do whatever you command, but I have offended the lady Blanchefleur. I did not know she was your daughter when I did it."

The King frowned. "When you did what?"

"I misunderstood my mother's directions, sire. I..."

"Well?"

Perceval looked around at the solemn knights, at his father, at the immortal queen of Avalon, and at Blanchefleur's august parents. "I kissed her," he mumbled, going red.

Sir Gawain's eyebrows reached for his hairline. A look of almost malicious pleasure crossed Sir Kay's face and he said, "Speak up, lad. I didn't hear you!"

The King looked at Nimue, who made some signal which

Perceval just missed. Then Arthur turned to the Queen and said, "Lady wife, do you remember what the penalty is for kissing a king's daughter? Something lingering, with molten lead in it, I think."

"I thought it was burning alive," said the Queen.

"No, no, that's for adultery."—"It was certainly lingering."

"I have promised to serve her a year and a day to repay her," Perceval said, stoic on the surface, although inside he was hot with shame. "But I think she might prefer it if you sent someone else, sire."

The King looked at him for so long that Perceval felt himself reddening once more. At length he stroked his beard again and said with a smile which Perceval did not understand, "If you have promised to serve her, then you had best keep your word. What do you say, Gawain?"

"I will ensure you can trust him, sire."

"Oh, I have no doubts about that. I meant whether you approve of his serving the lady Blanchefleur."

"Oh, *that!*" said Gawain. "No, sire. I wholeheartedly approve." And he too smiled, all white teeth, like the wolfhound under the King's chair.

"Guard her well, then," said the King to Perceval. "Remember that the fate of Logres may rest on your faithfulness in this."

"Sire," said Perceval, "if mortal man can guard your daughter, I will."

With this the council broke up, but as he went out of the solar Perceval felt a hand on his arm and turned to see the Lady Nimue.

"There are things you should know about the place you are going," she said. "Where can we speak?"

But when Perceval had led her to his chamber, which as

usual in Camelot did double duty as a sitting-room, she did not immediately begin to tell him of the other world where he would find the Lady Blanchefleur.

Instead she turned to him and said, "There is a thing it would be wise for you to know, son of Gawain."

Perceval bore up under the weight of her attention and said, "Say on."

"You are a newcomer to Camelot; indeed, to Logres," said Nimue. "Therefore you have not heard the stories about the birth of the damsel Blanchefleur."

"Stories?"

"For a time," the Lady said, looking at the ring on her finger, "it was whispered that the lady Queen loved Sir Lancelot."

The ring should have flattened to silver leaf between those adamant eyes and that stone-white hand. "No whisper ever reached my ears," he said.

"Spoken like the son of Gawain," and there was a mocking twist at the corner of her mouth. "But you have only come to Camelot today, true?"

Perceval said, "What is the point? You say this has something to do with the birth of the damsel Blanchefleur. Is she not the King's daughter? Is that what you mean?"

"Hush!" said Nimue, and her look hit him like a slap. "I mean to say nothing of the kind. Only that such was said once, before Sir Ector took her to the other world. Therefore, whatever lies in the damsel Blanchefleur's future at Camelot, I am sure that these stories will come to her ears. In that day, as in this, she may need a protector."

"But the King doesn't doubt she is his daughter. Does he?"

Nimue's eyes opened innocently, more like a mortal's, now, in their blank candour. "The King believes the Queen."

Perceval was suddenly angry with her. "You make him sound like a fool."

"Do I? I do not mean to. Whatever Arthur Pendragon is, he is no fool." She tilted her head. "Nor is the Queen. But even a very great man may have his blindnesses."

"Not him."

"Yes, even him. If there is a thing I have learned in all my endless years, it is that every man is blind in some direction."

"And you think the Queen is his?"

"I think he would be slow to think ill of her, and slower to think ill of Lancelot, and slowest of all to charge the most beloved knight of Logres with treason. Even if he cared nothing for the Queen, even if the brotherhood of the Table were not founded in his heart's blood, not even the Pendragon can afford to make an enemy of a man like Lancelot."

Perceval's mouth went dry. He went and picked up the Queen's silver-and-glass cup from the chest by his bed. "But Lancelot does love her, doesn't he? The day this was stolen, he claimed the quest as if by right."

"Yes," said Nimue.

Perceval turned the fragile vessel over and over. "And the Queen? What would happen to her?"

"You heard it yourself," said the Lady of Lake. "She would be burned alive."

Chapter 11

If men should rise and return to the noise and time of the
tourney,
The name and fame of the tabard, the tangle of gules and gold,
Would these things stand and suffice for the bourne of a
backward journey,
A light on our days returning, as it was in the days of old?

Chesterton

"YOU REALLY ARE LEAVING, THEN?" SAID Kitty Walker.

"I might *have* to." Blanche swished at the long lush grass with
a stick, keeping her head bent. If she looked up, she would see
the imperious autumn larches, sulphur fretted with black and
grey, sitting in judgement on her sulky mood. "I'm sorry to
hear that Mr Corbin has gone to London. I particularly wanted
to see him."

Kitty said, "I'll be sure to give him your invitation when
he comes back in the morning. Blanche! How shall I get on
without you?"

"I expect you'll get on very well."

"Do you *want* to go? Oh, Blanche, and I was going to ask you
to come to Paris with me next year."

Blanche sighed and reached for another clump of grass.

122

"Of course I don't. But I haven't much choice. You'll come tomorrow night, won't you, and say goodbye?"

"For the dinner party? Of course I shall. But I refuse to say goodbye. Remember, it's my birthday party in a week. You must stay long enough for that, for everyone is coming down from London, and they will need *someone* brainy to talk to, or they will think us no better than Welshmen."

Blanche chivvied millipedes absent-mindedly. "If I'm still here, Kitty, I'll come to it. But I can't promise."

"Oh, *bella*," said Kitty, and hugged her. "Sir Ector has a heart of stone. Now I must run home before those clouds decide to rain again."

Blanche glanced through the larches at the sky. Red-and-gold needles sprang jubilantly into relief against the purple clouds. Blanche couldn't help smiling. "I had better do the same."

"Although *you* won't mind if it does rain." Kitty reached out and touched the thick woollen cloak Blanche had brought back with her from Carbonek. "I *must* have one of these, Blanche! It would hold off a downpour!"

Blanche laughed and wrapped the luxurious garment more closely around her. "I don't care to put it to the test. Goodbye!"

Kitty tripped back down the path to the village, and Blanche, walking with a long swinging step, passed on under the flaming larches. The afternoon darkened toward the slow twilight that comes on an overcast day, and the forest, which at first glowed in the gloom, lost its colour as the light faded.

Blanche came out from under the trees and began climbing the bald ridge behind the house. A wind sprang up and lashed at her hair with a scattering of idle raindrops. She put up her hood, toiled up the last few feet of slope, and stood on the ridge. Looking back, she saw a long streak of red-and-gold sky where the bank of cloud ended over the Welsh hills. East, down the slope at her feet, she saw the house nestled in its garden, marked at the front by a row of brown-leafed elms and behind by the dormant orchard.

Affection welled up in her at the sight of her home. It was a good place to come back to, in the dark, after tramping on the hills—or after sojourning in the high cold halls of Logres.

Over the thrumming wind, someone called her name.

Blanche wheeled. In the dim dusk, the grey-clad figure was hardly visible against the hillside. As he came closer, something about his loping stride warned her that he was not from her own time. But up here on the hill there was nowhere to run. Blanche stood her ground until he was close enough for her to see his face.

"You again!" she whispered, and put a hand to her heart, which began to hammer now that the threat was past.

Sir Perceval inclined his head. "The King sent me," he said.

"How you frightened me!" said Blanche. Then, as she remembered her manners with a rush: "I am so sorry. I mean, good evening. But why have you come?"

"The King sent me," repeated Perceval, raising an eyebrow.

"For what?" Blanche took a second look at him and felt a wild impulse to laugh. Mail and surcoat were laid aside, and he was now correctly garbed in coat, waistcoat, and trousers. But they fitted badly, and the fault was exaggerated by his brown face and rumpled hair, which the buttons and starch only made look wilder.

Perceval said, "The Lady of the Lake has taken Sir Ector and her damsel to speak to the King. I have come to guard you in their place. They have told your people that I am your cousin, which is partly true."

It took Blanche a moment to realise that by *her people* Perceval meant the servants. To her, they were only the help. Blanche said: "Do you believe there is danger, then? Here?"

"We hope not," he said with a smile.

"But Morgan le Fay knows where I live."

He nodded. "The Lady says her rift has been repaired. But we do not know her full power, and Sir Ector has been called away." He grinned. "Do not fear. I am here to serve you, as I promised."

Despite the fit of schoolgirl giggles that had seized her in Carbonek when he first proposed to be her knight, his assurance annoyed her now. "You inspire me with almost perfect confidence," she said, honey-sweet. "With a few more years and experience, you would make a capable guardian, I'm sure."

"And you an amiable ward," he said, bowing again.

He spoke so courteously that Blanche had walked on five steps before she realised that he had insulted her. "I'm sure you were the obvious choice," she said, gesturing to the house below as it sat snug in its garden glowing with light, "given the magnitude of the present danger."

"The present danger, which is that the Witch of Gore, as you say, knows where you live."

Blanche shuddered and thought it a rather brutal reminder. They went on in silence, but now the house below seemed less comforting and more ephemeral, and the cold wind blowing against them reminded her of the void between the worlds, into which, as the horrible premonition struck her, it was the doom of all such pleasant and homely places to fall forever.

Would Night swallow them all in the end?

"But you are willing to risk your life for me?" she said at last, more earnestly.

Perceval repeated the words he had spoken in the King's solar.

"If mortal strength can save you, I will."

They reached the gate to the orchard. Blanche watched Perceval open it, the hair on the back of her neck prickling to remind her what had happened last time she and Nerys had crossed that portal. When they had passed safely into the orchard, and the gate was closed, Blanche said, "Why?"

"Why...?"

"Why will you..." she grimaced at the theatrical words "...save me?"

"The King—"

"The King sent you. I know."

They walked on between the shadows of the apple-trees. Blanche tried again.

"Aren't you afraid of what is coming?"

He laughed. "Pshaw!"

"What, do you like the—the pain, and the idea of dying?"

Perceval said: "No. But it is better than the idea of a life without any kind of danger, without any kind of victory."

Blanche shuddered. "Everyone fears death. What makes you so eager to face it?"

"I had rather keep my word sworn to you in Carbonek, and obey my King, than prove myself faithless." He thought a moment. "So I find that I am afraid, but of something worse than death."

That made her laugh. "Worse than death! Thanks! You are very comforting!"

They came through the gate at this side of the orchard and

into the garden. Perceval said, "Does it trouble you, having me here?"

"No," Blanche admitted. Then, after a moment, she said, "Shall I tell you what I think?"

He bent his head in assent.

"Each time I have gone to Logres, or needed help, you were there. It reminds me of what Vicar says, about Providence. I always thought it was a nice way of saying that everything is for the best. But after the last few months, how can I think that?"

"You know what destiny looks like," said Perceval at last.

"I do now."

"A mysterious plan, too strange to be happenstance. I too see it unfolding around us."

Blanche said: "But that is what frightens me. What seems best to Providence horrifies *me*. What if it takes me far away from home? What if it drives me into deeper danger? What if it…" she swallowed, "what if it wants to hurt me?"

They came out onto the lawn below the house, where light streamed out onto the grass, and Perceval looked at her. "Why, damsel," he said, with surprise and ineffable disappointment in his voice, "are you afraid?"

"Yes, terribly"—she bit back the words and glanced back the way they had come. The last light had faded out of the west and even the trees hardly seemed blacker than the sky. "I am sorry," she said at last. "The darkness made me afraid. In the light I will be brave enough."

Perceval looked out at the night and his answer, when it came, shook her. "I know what you mean by fearing the dark," he said. "The tales I heard of Logres spoke of it as a beacon of light. But I found it sieged by shadows." He glanced back at Blanche. "I,

127

too, fear the future. I fear that Logres is doomed to flicker and die, leaving only the dark, and that nothing I can do will stop it."

Blanche stared at him. "Do you mean that Logres is in danger?"

"It has always been in danger," he replied, with a smile.

"From Morgan le Fay?"

Perceval shook his head. "She is only the foremost of our enemies. Britain is full of sorcerers, barbarians, brigands, raiders, and rebels. It is the work of the Round Table to resist and subdue them, to shield the little people against them. Had you not heard this?"

"I—" Blanche began, and then fell silent. She could not truthfully say she had been ignorant of it, and suddenly, sickeningly, she was ashamed of herself. "I had heard it," she said, in a voice she hardly recognised. She laid her hand on Perceval's arm. "But what are you going to do about it?"

He smiled encouragingly. "The task at hand. The King said that the fate of Logres rests on your safety."

"That's what the prophecy said. But how?"

"You are his heir," said Perceval. "The one who will inherit Logres when he is gone. The one who will fend off the night. But you knew this too."

"I did," she said in horror. "But I never thought of it this way before. I never knew what was at stake." For a moment, the evening dark pressed in like the enemies of Logres; ahead, the windows of her own house gave off a comforting glow.

Blanche looked Perceval in the eye. "I am mortified," she said. "Here I have been telling you my own selfish woes, while you are trying to save a civilisation."

Perceval opened his mouth to speak, but there was the sound

of a gong from within the house.

"It is dinner," said Blanche with a shaky laugh. "Let us go in."

IN THE LIGHT, AS SHE HAD predicted, she felt stronger. It was good modern gaslight streaming from lamps mounted on the wall, and with the addition of a good solid butler like Keats to fill glasses and pass plates, Blanche felt even better. But the vision which had filled her imagination a moment ago on the lawn, of a kingdom besieged by primeval chaos, still weighed on her mind.

She fought it with forced mirth.

"So the railway has your box, Cousin Percy," she said in Welsh as Keats swam in with the soup. "You had better hope they disgorge it soon, or you will be wearing Sir Ector's clothes all the way back to Merthyr Tydfil. Our gentlemen's outfitter in the village is not the thing at all."

"No, not the thing," said Perceval, playing along valiantly, although he evidently did not understand one word in three.

"When we have a moment, you must tell me all the news. Thank you, Keats." Blanche took a feverish spoon of soup and was grateful that Perceval had apparently learned some table manners in the last few months.

Perceval spoke. "They say the new Bishop of Trinovant nearly burned down the cathedral by mistake during the winter."

"My goodness," said Blanche. "How extraordinary. Keats, will you close the curtains over there? I feel the dark coming in. The cold," she corrected herself, and afterwards fell silent.

After dinner, in the drawing room, Perceval wandered to the corner and inspected the bookshelves. Blanche sat down at the piano and tinkled a few bars of the *Well-Tempered Clavier*. Surprised, the knight whipped around to see what had caused the strange noise. Then he relaxed and came off guard like a dog coming off point, grinning as though he hadn't convinced her for a terrifying moment that some enemy had silently entered the room behind her.

Blanche banged the lid shut over the keys.

Perceval held up a book. "Tell me what this is."

"It's a book." She took it off him and flipped it open. "See inside? Writing."

He peered at it. "The little words. I never learned the trick of them."

"You never learned to *read?*"

He shook his head. "We had no books in the cave. And no parchments."

"The cave!" Blanche pressed her hand to her forehead.

He laughed and gestured to the piano. "It had no lamps or singing machines, but it was warm if you kept the fire going."

She had to let go of her dismay and laugh. "No, no, I'm sure it was lovely. Only I just remembered that the dinner party is tomorrow night. And you were brought up in a cave."

"Yes."

She said: "Well, at least Emmeline and I can speak Welsh. And at least the Welsh have a reputation for being half-savage, because I think we're going to need it."

BLANCHE SWISHED ACROSS THE HALLWAY AND tapped on the door of the room that had once been Sir Ector's. Silence. She tapped again. "It's me."

"I think," said Perceval from within, "you had better help me with this gorget."

She opened the door and found him struggling with his collar. "Do try to remember what I told you," she said, brushing away

130

his hands and pinning the collar on. "Say how-do-you-do to the guests, watch which forks and spoons I use, and avoid all subjects of religion and politics. There's the bell. They're here."

Kitty Walker and Emmeline Felton were in the hall removing wraps and hats when Blanche and Perceval came downstairs to meet them.

"Blanche, you look *delicious*," said Kitty, kissing the air by Blanche's cheeks. She glanced at Perceval. "Why, you coy thing, you never told me you were expecting anyone *else!*"

"I wasn't," Blanche said repressively. "This is a cousin from Merthyr Tydfil, Perceval de Gales. He only speaks Welsh."

Kitty looked at Perceval and giggled and said, "*Noswaith dda.*"

"Good evening," said Perceval in the same language.

Blanche hissed in English, "I thought you didn't speak Welsh?"

"Welsh nanny," said Kitty. She switched back to Welsh, sidling up to Perceval. "I haven't spoken the language for years. Do tell me if I say anything very funny."

Blanche sighed. "Hello, Emmeline dear."

The Vicar's daughter squeezed her affectionately and said, "I am so sorry you are going away, Blanche. We'll miss you."

"Oh, Emmeline, and I never thought—I'll miss your wedding. If I'm still here when Mr Pevensie comes back from London next week, you must bring him to visit."

Keats ushered in Mr Corbin in immaculate evening dress. The sight of him threw Blanche into confusion. She had meant to ask his advice. Kitty had probably let him know that she urgently wanted to speak to him. But now that she stood face to face with him, she had another twinge of conscience. She'd already told him about Logres, about her parents, about everything. She did not have the time to reason it through;

131

only sudden doubt hit her that it had been wise to reveal so much.

"Don't fib!" Kitty's delighted voice sliced through the hall, startled back into English. Blanche turned to see her dissolving in helpless laughter. "Blanche, darling, he says there are dragons in Wales."

Perceval laughed along with Kitty, as if enjoying her mirth. Blanche stood wordless.

"They *are* more difficult to find than they used to be," he said to Kitty in Welsh. "The giants, on the other hand, grow more numerous." She went off into fresh peals of laughter.

"Miss Pendragon, good evening," said Mr Corbin's soft amused voice at her side. "Where did you find such an original?"

She turned to him, forcing a smile. "M-my—" and then she caught herself. This man had nothing to do with Logres, and her guardian and Nerys had gone to great lengths to keep the servants and others in Gloucestershire from knowing where they had come from. Her conscience nudged again, and she heard herself continuing smoothly:

"A friend of my guardian's, come down to keep me company. Percy de Gales. Of the Merthyr Tydfil de Gales."

"Will you introduce us?" said Mr Corbin.

"Oh, I'd love to, although he doesn't speak English."

"That need not hinder us," said Mr Corbin in perfect Welsh.

Blanche stared. "I suppose you had a Welsh nanny too, then," she said feebly.

"No," he said, smiling. "My nanny was a woman from Carlisle. But I learned the language years ago conducting a study on conditions in a Welsh ordnance factory. And now I'd very much like to meet your friend."

There was nothing to do but lead him over and make the introduction. "Percy, this is Mr Simon Corbin. He—what *do* you call the profession, Mr Corbin?—he writes letters to *The Times* about education reform."

Blanche, watching the two of them exchange politenesses, wondered if it could be possible to find two more dissimilar men. Even the tentative air she detected in Perceval, as he tried to conceal his ignorance of Gloucestershire manners, could not veil his open face or chill his laughing eyes like the mocking and secretive melancholy of Mr Corbin.

Then Keats appeared to announce dinner, and Blanche asked Mr Corbin to escort Emmeline. Kitty took Perceval's arm. He solemnly offered the spare to Blanche, and she took it, the better to surpervise his conduct on the way into the dining-room.

Entrée and soup. Kitty, making desultory conversation with Perceval, wanted to know if he had been up to Llanstephan at all, and didn't he adore the little town? Perceval said No, but fame of its beauty had spread throughout Merthyr Tydfil and the countries around. Emmeline was talking to Mr Corbin about the war, in Welsh for courtesy's sake.

Main course, lamb cutlets. "I don't think it's right at all," Emmeline was saying. "Poisoning the wells, burning the houses, and shutting up the women and children in camps? This is not a just war."

Mr Corbin smiled. "How else do you propose we shall win, Miss Felton? We are fighting a mobile and well-supplied guerrilla force. The Boers buzz about our ears like gnats, and while the generals make futile attempts to swat them, hundreds of men are dying of typhoid."

Emmeline looked beseechingly at Blanche. But Mr Corbin went on: "You think me heartless, Miss Felton, but I assure you

I am not. The families in the camps are being cared for; outside, they would only starve. Meanwhile, it behoves us to take every advantage in this struggle. Is it not better to win at once and end the suffering, than to continue locked in stalemate?"

Emmeline bowed her head, but said, "If the Boers thought so, they would already have surrendered."

"If the Boers thought so, there would not have been a war," said Mr Corbin with a laugh. "In a perfect world these sad decisions would be unnecessary."

Perceval had been following the conversation, and now he spoke. "Yet in fighting, as in anything else, Christian warriors must act in accordance with their prayers. *Adveniat regnum tuum sicut in caelo et in terra.*"

"Christians? Mr Corbin is a *nonbeliever*, Percy," said Kitty with a laugh.

Mr Corbin raised a conciliatory hand. "Yet I understand you, I think, sir. You mean that the citizens of heaven must act as though they were in heaven. But this is my point. God knows—if He exists—where heaven is, but it certainly is not on the earth."

"Augustine says—" Blanche began to object, but Mr Corbin had not finished.

"This is the real world, sir. Save your ideals for heaven."

"I say that a battle which cannot be won without treachery and dishonour is a battle not worth winning."

"It is a pretty idea, certainly," said Mr Corbin with a smile which even Blanche thought was rather provoking. "But *I* think that if you were a fighting man, de Gales, you would find the model difficult to put into practice."

"It can be done," said Perceval, sitting back in his chair with arrogant ease and folding his arms.

"Can it? Let us try it ourselves, now. Cast me as the villain in a melodrama, de Gales. Having crippled you with a cowardly blow, I turn to condemn one of these adorable ladies—" he turned with half a bow to Kitty, who giggled—"Miss Walker, for instance, to death, or a fate worse. I twirl my moustache. Miss Walker faints. And you, sir, recollect that you have a weapon concealed on your person."

Perceval shifted in his seat. Blanche read his face like a book. Oh dear. He *did* have a weapon concealed on his person.

"Do not deny, Mr de Gales, that to preserve her you would take your last chance. You would bury your knife in my back without a second thought, without a warning, no matter how unchivalrous that might be."

Perceval, less arrogant now, stared mutely at the table. At last he stirred and said, "It would depend—"

"Sophistry, sir!" Mr Corbin thundered. He went on: "Ah, but even now you fail to understand me. What if it were not the villain doing these dastardly deeds, but your colleague, or your commander?"

Perceval looked up with quick displeasure. "What do you mean?"

"I mean," he said, "that by your own showing, the greatest threat to heaven comes from within the ranks of the angels themselves. Before you can prove to me that heroes can defeat villains with nothing but the purest chivalric ideals, you must convince me that heroes do exist, and that villains are not a fanciful tale for children. You must tell me, sir, if you dare, that you are incorruptible, and that your colleagues and commanders are as pure as you. Your health."

And Mr Corbin took a sip of wine. Perceval, with a furious scowl, stared at his plate. Blanche herself was suddenly angry with the schoolmaster. It hadn't been a fair fight; Mr Corbin was so much older and so much more worldly than Perceval. But she could not take up the argument on his behalf. For one thing, she had been lax in her duties as a hostess in not diverting the conversation sooner. And for another, if she was honest, she was inclined to agree with Mr Corbin.

She searched in vain for some lighthearted joke to dispel the blunt force of his words. But nothing came, and she rather awkwardly said, "Tell us what you have planned for your birthday, Kitty."

LATER, IN THE DRAWING-ROOM, BLANCHE SAT alone with her cup of tea. Emmeline was at the piano, playing country airs, and Perceval stood with his head inside the instrument, asking questions and keeping Kitty in giggles. Under the music, the hum of voices, and the laughter, Mr Corbin came over to sit on the stool by Blanche's feet.

"Let me have your reproaches," he said to her in English. "You will not find me unrepentant."

Blanche tried to determine whether he was joking or not, but failed, as usual, to read his expression. "It was very wrong of you."

"Poor lad," he said, smiling. There was a moment's silence, and he went on, "He is not from the Wales we know, is he?"

Even if she had wanted to lie, Blanche's face would have given her away. "No."

"Perhaps I am jealous of them," said Mr Corbin, under the piano's melody, so low that she had to lean forward to hear. "Those half-savage warlords and unwashed illiterates who would take you away from us."

"I—" Blanche's protest died away.

"Your guardian told us you had gone on holiday," Mr Corbin probed. "I didn't believe it. You went *there*."

She gave him a look of mute appeal.

"Remember," he said, "they can't force you to live there. It's your choice."

He was going to try to prevent her going to Logres if he could. She supposed she should be grateful for his help. But a sudden unease gripped her, a feeling like a bad conscience.

"I used to dream," she said, and swallowed. "I dreamed I was there, in a meadow with the sun shining on banners and armour. And it wasn't like what you say. It was beautiful." She remembered the night in the slough in Gore, when in cutting wind she had determined to die uncomplaining, with her face to the free hills, and tried to put the splendour of that moment into words. "Now that I know such a place exists, I can't help wondering...*what if it is true?*"

"Blanche, no."

"What if they need me?"

"*Need* you? Blanche, who has been worrying you?"

"No-one," she said, bewildered.

"Don't make the best of a bad bargain, my dear."

He was still fighting for her. She felt a quick rush of gratitude, and dropped her voice. "I can't think of any way to avoid it. Besides—"

And she caught herself.

"Besides?"

"It's nothing."

"You said, 'What if they need me'. They can't need you to destroy yourself by flinging yourself into their brutal world."

"But what if they do?" He looked puzzled. She tried again. "If my sacrifice can preserve them—"

"Someone else will do it."

"They said—" This time, although she caught herself, she permitted herself to go on. She glanced at Perceval and dropped her voice a little lower. "They said they need me."

"Nonsense. They'll make do with someone else. Besides, to them, you're only a woman. How important can it be?"

"I'm to guard the Holy Grail."

Mr Corbin's lips pressed together and turned white. "So," he said at last, "not content with spiriting you away to primitivism, they're making you the high priestess of their bogus cult."

"I—"

"Blanche, look at me and tell me that if there was a way to stay, you wouldn't take it."

"I—"

"I can find a way. Tell me you aren't interested, and you need never see me again."

"It would depend on the way," she whispered at last.

"Then promise me you won't go before you've seen me again," he said.

Chapter 12

It's I will keep me a maiden still,
Let the elfin knight do what he will.
Lady Isabel and the Elf-Knight

THE DAYS STRETCHED OUT WITH NO sign of Sir Ector and Nerys. Kitty was busy on her party business, and Mr Corbin did not call again. There was little to do that week except to amuse Perceval, but he took a great deal of amusing. Hitherto Blanche had been glad to muddle through life doing a little reading, a little handiwork, and a little visiting, but Perceval could not read, visit, or tat, and quickly grew restless without work to do. For most of the day he occupied himself working with the horses. Sir Ector had ridden Malaventure to Logres, but Perceval spent hours riding in circles on Rufus and Florence, training them to respond to the lightest pressure of rein or heel and gaining balance and rhythm for himself. Then he rigged up a makeshift quintain for ring jousting, and pounded white-painted wooden pegs into the ground which, approaching at a gallop, he aimed to spear and carry away.

In the evenings, Blanche found him a knife and knots of wood to whittle while she read aloud, mostly in Latin, and they had far-ranging conversations as knotted bowls or dragon-handled spoons took shape under Perceval's hands.

"How much longer do you think Sir Ector will be?" Blanche asked one evening in the drawing-room.

Perceval kept all his attention on the wood in his hands, a block of dark walnut. "Time flows differently here than in Logres. But I know it will take them a week of that time to travel from Nimue's gate to Camelot and return."

"So if time moves more slowly here, which it seemed to do while I was at Carbonek, we may look for them in a little under a week from now." Blanche stared into the fire and wondered if she would get the chance to speak to Mr Corbin again before she left.

She said, "Do you think Mr Corbin was right, about the necessities of war?"

"No," Perceval said, frowning at the walnut. His knife scraped against the wood three times before he asked it, the question she'd been hoping to avoid. "What did you talk to him about, the other night?"

"He doesn't want me to leave," she said at last.

"Why should he have a say in it?"

Blanche laughed. "You really don't like him, do you?" she baited.

Perceval didn't take the hook. "He bested me in argument," he admitted. "But he was wrong."

"He made me promise to see him again before I leave." Blanche was probing in earnest now, wondering what Perceval's reaction to this would be. But once more he spoke calmly:

"He will be at the damsel Kitty's dance three days from now, surely. There's no reason you should not speak to him then, if the Lady tarries."

Blanche wondered if Perceval really was not suspicious of Mr

140

Corbin's intentions. But she let it lie, and because Kitty's party was to be a fancy-dress affair, she began mentally searching her wardrobe for a costume.

KITTY'S ROEDEAN FRIENDS CAME DOWN FROM London for the occasion, and Blanche, entering the ballroom on Perceval's arm, felt Kitty had done due honour to the splendour of the occasion. The place was blazing with light reflected from silverware and crystal, decorated with tinsel and silk roses.

"It's marvellous, isn't it?" Kitty asked. She was dressed as a fairy princess, with gossamer wings and a glittering crown. "Mamma let me do what I liked. We had Madame de Lorraine come down to decorate. Ooh, Percy, what a wonderful costume! Where did you get it?" she added in Welsh.

"My aunt Lynet made the surcoat," Perceval said, which was perfectly true. "Many Happy Returns."

"And who are you, Blanche?"

"Marie-Antoinette."

"Is that why there's an hourglass around your neck?" Kitty screamed. "Oh, how horrid! And you must be Sir Lancelot, Percy."

Perceval glanced down at his glittering mail and red-and-gold surcoat. "Must I?"

Kitty clapped her hands. "Oh, excellent! 'Must I'! Did you hear, Simon?"

"Most amusing," said Mr Corbin, who had just come in, and showed his white teeth in tribute to the joke. He gave Kitty his best wishes, and then moved on to Blanche and bowed.

"Good evening," she said, giving him her hand. "And whom do you represent, Mr Corbin? The Duke of Wellington?"

"His nemesis, I'm afraid."

141

"Napoleon Bonaparte!" Blanche withdrew her hand with a laugh. "I don't know if I can shake hands with you, sir."

"Simon, ask her for that ghastly hourglass as a keepsake," Kitty, who had been welcoming other guests, interjected.

Mr Corbin looked at the pendant and smiled his secretive smile. "I shall ask her for a good deal more than that tonight."

Blanche glanced at Perceval, a little guiltily. But of course he had not heard: the thing was said in English.

"To begin with," Mr Corbin went on, "this waltz."

Blanche said, "Excuse me," to Perceval and allowed Mr Corbin to lead her onto the floor.

"I am not a good dancer," he said, a smile crossing his melancholy face—Blanche murmured a polite disagreement—"But I know that when one has an assignation at a ball, one puts pleasure before business."

They moved into the flow of couples. Mr Corbin had been quite correct. The pleasure would be all his: of the two of them, he had the better partner. Blanche relaxed and let him guide her where he wished. There would be more opportunities for dancing later.

"We make a pretty picture, I'm sure," she said. "The last of the *ancien regime* and the first of the new."

"Thesis and antithesis," Mr Corbin said. "What comes next is synthesis."

They threaded a narrow passage between two other couples and drifted on up the room. Blanche said: "I have heard of this before. The thesis is received doctrine. The antithesis is some new and revolutionary idea. And the synthesis—"

"Is what happens when thesis and antithesis marry."

"And I thought philosophy was unromantic," said Blanche, smiling.

The music ended. Mr Corbin snatched a pair of champagne *coupes* and offered his arm to Blanche. "Now for the business. Shall we step outside, onto the terrace?"

It was a clear, cold night, and Blanche, folding her arms, hoped the discussion would not take long. "How cold it is!" she said, glancing at the moon.

"Winter is trying her teeth," Mr Corbin said. "But tonight she is only a pup: when she is old, ware her bite."

Blanche turned to him with an inquiring shiver. "I promised not to go away without seeing you."

"And I promised to find you a way to stay in this world, if you chose to take it."

"Tell me."

He said with more than his usual solemnity, "I hope you do choose to take it, Blanche. I don't wish to lose you."

He should not have been using her Christian name, Blanche thought. But another shiver of excitement and cold danced down her spine, and she thought she knew what was coming.

"Blanche Pendragon, will you join me in my life's work? Will you forsake your guardians and homeland, and join your purpose with mine? In a word, will you marry me, and free yourself to claim a new heritage, a new world bright with the hope of reason and brotherhood?"

He spoke with gleaming eyes, and lips that curved in a smile as the words rolled from them. It was what Blanche had expected—but not quite what she had expected, and a faint cloud of disappointment fell over her. She had dreamed of being addressed in an enraptured whisper, not in measured apostrophes like the lines in a play.

Still, perhaps the tender passion struck some men differently.

"I hardly know what to say," she said. "Dare I?"

"As my wife, you would be answerable only to me—and that only if you wished," said Mr Corbin. "You would be protected not only from the will of your guardians but also from the diplomatic marriage they no doubt intend for you."

Blanche paled. "That hadn't occurred to me."

"Blanche," he was saying, "do you hear me? I am offering you a sure way to defy your fate. And my entire regard and affection into the bargain."

Blanche stood motionless, speechless, as though suddenly deprived of will. *Did* she want to marry Simon Corbin? Three months ago, she would have thought she did; she would not have cared that it would break Sir Ector's heart. *Did* she want to escape the burden of Logres? A week ago, she had—before Perceval had come, and unmasked her for a selfish coward.

The consent was trembling on her lips. But when she spoke, in a suddenly choked voice, she surprised herself as well as Mr Corbin.

"I can't."

"Can't what?" he cried. "Cannot defy the selfishly-imposed will of a family you've never seen? Cannot free yourself from the superstitions of barbarism?"

Blanche put her hands to her head. "I despise myself, but not for that. When I thought I had no choice, I bemoaned my lot with the satisfaction that I would be forced to do the right thing in the end. Now you present me with an alternative, and I say...I say that I thank you, Simon, and beg your forgiveness. I have trifled with you. I have allowed you to make this declaration, when I should have known that I could never accept it."

She fidgeted with the hourglass around her neck and looked at him timidly, sure that he would be hurt and offended. But his face had not changed. Only his voice became challenging.

144

"Why not?"

She would have had to fight to abandon Logres. Now her indecision had guaranteed that she would have to fight to go there, and she knew she had only herself to thank. "I should have known that I could never grieve my guardian so," she said, lifting her chin. "Then…we are not suited to each other. Our difference of outlook would keep us from agreeing, and besides, there is the question of my duty to Logres."

"None of these things need bind you," he said. "If you will not marry me, let me spirit you away to some place where they will not find you."

"I don't expect you to understand," she said with a strained smile. "You have put a choice before me, my friend. And I am grateful. But I choose to be bound. I will go to Logres, and do what is asked of me."

"So be it," he said gloomily. "We shall lose you, and Blanche Pendragon will be known no more among her friends and cavaliers."

Blanche remembered the pendant around her neck. She tugged the ribbon loose and held it out to him.

"I think you had better take it back. Remember me by it, if you like."

Simon Corbin took the hourglass from her hand and held it up to the moonlight. A bitter smile curled his lips.

"It has run its course," he said, and dropped it underfoot and crushed it into the pavement.

Blanche drew a swift breath of shock at the sudden controlled violence of his movement. But she had no time to speak, for Kitty's voice frothed out of the ballroom followed in a moment by herself.

"Simon! Yoo-hoo, Simon!" When she saw Blanche standing

there with Mr Corbin, Kitty put her hands to her mouth with a gasp. "Oh! I am so sorry! It's nothing, really."

Behind Kitty stood Perceval, a tall upright figure, mail-shirted, with his sword swinging from his hip. After the last five minutes, the sight of him was as welcome as reinforcements in the heat of battle, and her shoulders dropped in relief. She looked past Mr Corbin, past Kitty, and smiled at him.

"Don't wait for me, Mr Corbin," she said in Welsh.

He bowed to her and offered his arm to Kitty. They passed into the ballroom and Perceval came forward to lean against the baluster of the terrace beside her.

"I see you have spoken to him," he said.

"I have," she said. "I keep no secrets from you, my deputed guardian. Mr Corbin has made me a proposal of marriage, and I have refused him."

"This was his attempt to keep you here?"

She smiled sadly. "He said that if I married him, I would be able to defy Sir Ector. I said I chose not to do it. He was angry, I think."

Perceval laughed. "Let us not mind him."

His dismissive tone grated on Blanche. She had cherished Simon Corbin's good opinion. She had even, once or twice, dreamed of accepting him. Did Perceval think it was an easy thing to spurn such a man's protection? Did he think that the choice was so obvious, between the dangers and hardships of Logres, and the comfort and freedom of her home?

"I am sorry I had to do it," she said in a sharper voice. "If my fate were any different, I should be glad to have him."

Perceval looked incredulous. "Be glad your fate is wiser than you, then."

"Oh!" said Blanche, "just because you lost an argument to

him, you must act as though no woman could like him."

"What?" Perceval yelped. "I deny it. Someone may someday love that dirgeful face, but never you."

Blanche could not think of a good retort, so she snapped open her fan and turned to re-enter the ballroom. But Perceval called her back, gently. "Lady. Stay a moment."

He rose from the terrace baluster, and took her hand. "I did not come to quarrel with you, Blanchefleur."

She did not trust herself to speak, and therefore only raised an eyebrow.

"Forget about Simon Corbin. Look elsewhere for one who would serve you and guard you."

"To you, of course." But his earnestness disarmed her, and the words came out with less hiss and spit than she wished.

"Yes, to me." His thumb traced over the back of her fingers and touched the red-gold ring of Ragnell. "I told you once that I saw a kind of destiny in our acquaintance."

"Please don't…"

"It was you and no-one else in the pavilion, in the courtyard, and at Carbonek," he said. "You are perilous and fair. Is it any wonder you should run in my mind?"

Blanche stared back at him for a long moment, her mind a whirl of conflicting thoughts. "Why, Perceval," she said at last with a shaky laugh, "are you jealous of him?"

The earnestness slipped away from him, and he laughed. "Jealousy implies doubt," he said with the boundless arrogance she detested. "I never doubted you for a moment."

Blanche flushed. "Doubt me? What right could you have had to doubt me? What am I? Your sweetheart?"

The instant the word was out of her mouth, Blanche could have bit her tongue off with mortification. Perceval looked down at her and slowly smiled, a dog's smile, all teeth.

"Are you?"

"Don't be odious. Of course not," she snapped, more vexed with herself than with Perceval. "It was a figure of speech. I mean," she went on, less angrily, "you and I would *never* suit. We do not share an intellectual level at *all*. And please don't bring up that scene in the pavilion again. I thought we decided to forget the whole business."

Perceval stuck his thumbs in his belt and whistled. "Oh, lady, be kind," he said, and grinned.

He opened the door for her to return to the ballroom, and she passed through with trailing robes of displeasure. But if he felt it, he gave no sign.

Chapter 13

Therewith the Giant buckled him to fight,
Inflam'd with scornful wrath and high disdain,
And lifting up his dreadful club on hight,
All arm'd with ragged snubs and knotty grain,
Him thought at first encounter to have slain.
Spenser

FOUR MORE DAYS PASSED, AND PERCEVAL spent less time with the horses and more time pacing around the house, watching the hills.

"Are they late, Perceval?" Blanchefleur asked him one morning as she saw him pass the library windows for the second time.

He opened the French doors and wandered in, frowning. "I cannot tell."

"I'm sure someone will come eventually," she said with resolute cheerfulness.

"Yes," he said, "the Lady—or the Lady's bane."

"What does that mean?"

"It means, the thing that killed her." And he prowled out by another door.

The following afternoon Emmeline and her young man

visited. Blanche felt the cloud lift. They went with the sun, and so did the brief gaiety they had brought with them. That night was cold and clear, with stars glittering overhead. Dinner was hushed. Perceval ate sparingly, coiled like a spring, Blanche thought.

"If they do not come tomorrow," Perceval said, "we must forestall them and take a door to Logres."

"The wardrobe in the hall goes to Carbonek," said Blanche.

"Only with the right elf-key, I think. The damsel Nerys left it with me. We'll take it tomorrow."

Blanche retired early, but found sleep beyond her. She turned up the lamp and settled in with Augustine. For hours there was no sound but the periodic chime of the downstairs clock, which struck nine o'clock, ten o'clock, and a quarter to twelve before she began to feel sleepy.

It was nearly midnight when Blanche heard the wind. It came screaming from the west like a bird of prey and gripped and shook the house. Blanche listened to it for a moment with puzzlement, then rolled over again and went back to reading. She had ceased to hear the storm when there was a tap and the door creaked open. It was Perceval, armed *cap-a-pie* with his sword drawn, moving more quietly in his steel harness that she would have thought possible.

"What's wrong?" Blanche gasped, rising and snatching the woollen cloak from Carbonek.

"Softly," he said; but he moved quickly and had pulled her halfway to the door before she could draw breath.

"Don't—give me a moment," Blanche whispered, struggling.

She went to turn back, but Perceval caught both her wrists and wrapped his arms around her. There was a noise like thunder and the outside wall of the bedroom exploded inward.

150

Blanche screamed. Huge jagged shards of glass from the window sank into the wall around them. Through the gaping void, Blanche saw stars in the sky. Then the raging wind whipped her hair across her face and blinded her.

Perceval, whose armoured body had shielded her from the blast, was speaking in a murmur. "Listen," he said. "Get the servants out of the house—out the front. I'll deal with the giant."

There was another rending crash and the corner of the room, with some of the floor, crumbled agonisingly away.

"Giant?" Blanche whimpered.

Perceval pushed her out the door, out of the wrecked room. She paused staring as he stepped to her bedside, picked up the heavy lantern, and smashed it against one of the bedposts. Burning oil rained across the coverlet and melted into the carpet, caught and spread by the wind. He had no time to do more. A hand, horrifying merely for its hugeness, came out of the night, gripped the ragged broken wall, and strained. Then a massive figure, blacker than the sky itself, rose against the stars.

Perceval, lifting his shield, sank into a crouch.

Blanche fled. Downstairs, some of the servants had already shuffled into the hall, blinking and yawning. Keats was there with a candle, and Lucy the housemaid, armed with a trembling poker. "Fire," Blanche gasped, before they could open their mouths. "Where's Cook? And John? And Daisy? We must all go at once."

She drove them before her out the front door into the storm.

THE GIANT CLAMBERED INTO BLANCHE'S ROOM, more than twice man-height, bent like an immense cloud to fit below the tall ceilings. A battle-axe like a short polearm, dagger-pointed at the end of the haft, dangled from one gnarled hand. Perceval, shifting from foot to foot, kept his eyes on it. The giant could not swing his weapon easily in the narrow confines of Blanche's room: when he saw the knight, he rammed the axe at him point-first.

Perceval slipped aside to avoid the dagger-point, stepped lightly onto the axe-blade as it whistled toward him, and launched himself forward. Behind, another wall splintered as the axe punched through. Perceval landed in a crouch under the giant's outstretched arm and swung back and lashed at the inside of the massive elbow. *Clank.* His blade, which should have bit deep and drunk, rebounded with a harsh whine; his arms jolted.

The creature was wearing armour.

The giant kicked. Perceval was already moving to the side, but it got him on the shield. The shock travelled up his arm, and Perceval thought he felt an old wound split open. He staggered back, falling to one knee. Then the giant wrenched his axe out of the wall: more plaster, dust, and splinters hummed through the frantic air. The flaming mass which had been Blanche's bed licked out a tongue of flame and ignited the dust. The whole room flashed with a puff of flame. Through it Perceval heard, rather than saw, the axe-blade come swinging toward him. He scrambled up and flung himself for a corner, the pain in his arm forgotten.

The axe bit into the wall next to him. Again, debris and flame filled the air, and the house groaned and trembled in the wind. Perceval knew he hadn't much time.

BLANCHE STOOD ON THE LAWN OUTSIDE the house,

152

watching the glowing windows.

"Is everyone here?" she yelled over the wind, trembling violently, but whether from cold or from fear she could not tell.

"I think—" said the cook uncertainly, and began counting on her fingers.

"I think the gas pipes behind the house must have blown," Blanche heard herself say. It was true, too, with half of the back wall smashed in. "It's dangerous—we must keep clear of the house."

John, the coachman, unlike the others, was alert and unpanicked. "I'll ride and fetch the fire brigade, miss."

"I suppose you had better," said Blanche, for she could think of nothing else to say. But if the fire brigade came at once, would Perceval have time to deal with the giant? "Wait," she called after him. "The horses! They are still in the stables! If the fire spreads—"

John and Keats set off for the stables.

"Miss, miss," gasped the cook, fighting the shawl she'd snatched to wrap around her, "Mr Perceval—he's not here."

Blanche looked at her, trying to think of something to say.

"He must be still in the house," said Daisy.

"I'll fetch him," the cook volunteered.

"No! You mustn't!" Blanche put her hands to her head. She could not tell them to sit back and watch the house burn down with someone still inside. And she certainly could not send anyone in after him.

There was only one thing to do.

"I'll go in and find him."

"No, don't!" sobbed Daisy. "I'll run for Mr Keats."

"Don't move," said Blanche, and turned the full force of her look on the housemaid; to her surprise, Daisy shrank back, looking almost frightened. But they had to obey her now; it was desperately important, and she had nothing but her voice and her eyes. She stiffened from crown to heel and said: "Listen, all of you. *Stay here*. I will fetch my cousin."

"But—" the cook protested.

"You can't. Not with the smoke, and your bronchitis. *Quiet!* You will obey me."

She had never spoken like this before. They stared at her dazedly, but they neither moved nor objected. She fixed them with one last glare, then turned and ran through the gale to the house. Her thoughts thrummed to the time of her feet:

"I must make a plan. I must make a plan."

PERCEVAL GROANED AND COUGHED, FLUNG OFF the flaming waste which had followed him into the depths, and rose unsteadily to his feet. He looked around. The floor of Blanche's room, once it collapsed, had dropped them among fiery wreckage into the library, and the bookshelves had blossomed into flame.

He was in poor case. His armour still kept him whole, but his right hand was scorched and the smell of singed hair, as well as improved visibility, told that his helm was gone. There was blood and smoke stinging his eyes; he rubbed and blinked the tears away.

Over in the corner, the colossal enemy reared to his knees and glanced around. Perceval, still shaking, lifted his shield, but the giant ignored him, climbed to his feet, and swung his axe at the wall.

Blanchefleur was the true quarry, and if that wall gave way the giant would be out of the house, free to move, able to snatch her and crush her in a moment. Perceval howled and lunged. The giant waited for him to come in range, then swung an iron fist. Perceval ducked to the floor, came up and jumped. The giant's armour was crude mail; there would be a chink somewhere. He clung to the massive body for only half a second before being brushed off, but in that half-second he stabbed deep into the giant's armpit. There was a bellowing roar and a shake that sent him tumbling across the room. The giant lifted his axe again.

Perceval was up and out of the way in the nick of time. Again he dashed in close, within the giant's reach, and circled round, drawing his poniard in his left hand. The long, slender knife, he hoped, would do the trick; he waited for the giant to straighten a little to turn, and then he plunged the blade screeching between the chain links of the creature's mail, into the back of the knee.

The giant bellowed again and his leg snapped shut with a convulsive kick, trapping Perceval's left hand in the hinge of the knee. He felt the bones in his hand grinding together and then the knee opened. He left the poniard wedged into the giant's mail and slithered to the ground.

So the enemy was crippled now, but savagely angry. Perceval snatched up his sword from the floor and ran into the corridor.

INSIDE THE HOUSE BLANCHE HEARD WUTHERING wind, roaring fire and the commotion of battle mixed into a thunderous symphony. Heavy smoke and flakes of paper gusted on the air.

In the hall she put her hands to her head and tried to think. Perceval had smashed her lamp and set fire to her room, either to help him defeat the giant or to destroy all signs of the fight.

Did he have a plan beyond survival? Blanche looked up at the wardrobe which led to Carbonek. On the other side of that door was safety and shelter and the Holy Grail. She dashed to it and pulled at the handle. Locked, and Perceval had the—elf-key, as he called it. Desperate, Blanche snatched up a letter-opener lying on the side-table by the front door. It only took her a moment to slide back the tongue of the lock and fling the door open.

Beyond hope she saw two narrow walls of rock running away into the darkness. There was a puff of cold, fresh air and the scent of earth. She could run away and be at Carbonek long before morning; it was only a short scramble down the rocks. Perceval would deal with the giant and, if he survived, be collected by Sir Ector and Nerys when they came.

She put a foot inside the wardrobe, onto the path. It flashed into her mind that Carbonek had a will of its own: it seemed not to need keys or even doors, it had yielded gracefully to a lock picked with a letter-opener—it wanted her, and its goodwill leapt toward her through the dark.

Yet still she hesitated. Then a flake of burning wallpaper drifted down from the upper landing, and the hall-carpet smouldered where it fell. Blanche peered up through the murk to see a flicker of red at the top of the stairs. Then there was another crash, and the house shook.

She found herself standing motionless, listening and waiting for the next sound. Was he still alive? There came a muffled bellow from the corridor that led down to the library. Yes. Blanche took one more longing look at the dark cleft inside the wardrobe and pushed the door to, propping it open with the paper-knife. Carbonek could wait for Perceval.

Blanche wrapped her cloak more closely around her, crossed

the hall and stepped into the corridor, full of thick choking smoke with a dull yellow glow at the end. She felt the house trembling around her with a succession of thumps. Then out of the halo of smoke Perceval appeared, running toward her. He had lost his helm, his surcoat was scorched and tattered, and his face was covered in soot.

He skidded to a stop when he saw her and almost stumbled into her arms. At the same moment, the library exploded into the corridor with an ear-shattering crash and a tide of wind and fire, and Perceval, regaining his feet, shouted, "Get out!"

He turned to face the giant. The massive enemy crawled into the passage, reaching out his hand, while the flaming walls groaned around his shoulders.

Perceval tightened his two-handed grip on his sword, hefted it to his shoulder, and ran. The outstretched hand snatched at him, but he swerved to one side and skidded under it on his knees. A look of foolish surprise crossed the giant's face as he realised that he had missed his tiny foe. Then Perceval plunged his blade into one stupefied eye.

All this had barely taken a few moments, and Blanche had not stirred. Thus she saw the death of the giant: a spurt of blood, the eyeball tumbling out, and the final, desperate struggle as it died.

Perceval wrenched his sword back and came reeling up the corridor to Blanche, scarcely evading the thrashing arm which tore through the walls and flung the fire further. Blanche stepped forward and caught him just as his knees buckled.

"Stand, sir," she commanded. "The house is falling. We must go."

They staggered out into the hall. There was fire here now, too, and Blanche, treading with thin slippers, sucked in her breath as something seared her foot. Perceval hardly seemed conscious and she had almost his full weight to bear. A short dash through the flames would take them to the wardrobe. Blanche hesitated, coughing, balancing on her unburned foot, trying to blink back the tears of pain. Then, just as she gathered herself to stagger forward, a sconce which hung from the high ceiling above fell crashing to the floor, followed within a heartbeat by the beam it hung from. The way was blocked.

Blanche cast one last despairing look at the wardrobe, barely visible through flame and smoke, then pulled Perceval's arm around her neck and half-dragged him a step or two to the back door. She fumbled with the latch. Then the door banged open, driven by the wind, and she staggered down the steps and into the garden.

In the biting gale, Perceval revived somewhat. "Further," he rasped. "Into the orchard."

They fell to the ground at last beneath a pear-tree, in grass wet with dew. Perceval groaned in pain as he relaxed. Blanche leaned back against the tree and gasped for breath. Here, at the foot of the rise behind the house, they were just high enough to see the whole place wrapped in flames, and the hills lit up with a lurid light.

"My home," she said. "And our door back to Logres!"

Perceval grunted in reply. Pain stabbed through Blanche's foot like a reminder and she turned to him in concern. "Are you badly hurt?"

He grinned. "I don't know."

Blanche clutched her hair. "Oh, what are we going to do? The wardrobe is gone and I can't *imagine* how I shall explain you to the servants."

"I still have the key," Perceval muttered. Then something

caught his attention. He struggled to his elbow and said, "Hark!"

It was a low rumble, shivering up from the ground. Blanche froze. Then, with a rolling, thunderous crash, the house collapsed. Yellow and scarlet flames shot up into the sky, illuminating everything. A moment later, when the glare died down somewhat, Blanche could see the little huddle of servants on the front lawn. There were John and Keats, holding the horses; there was Cook, fallen to her knees with her handkerchief to her mouth, and Lucy and Daisy clinging to each other in terror.

"They think we are dead," said Perceval, and fell back with a sigh. Blanche went to rise, but he raised his hand. "No," he said. "More trouble may come. Wait."

He fumbled for his sword, trying to wipe the blood off onto the grass. Blanche, seeing how it hurt him to move, said, "Let me." She cleaned the long blade gingerly, then slid it back into the scabbard.

"Let me see your hands," she told him, and eased the gauntlets off. His left hand was bruised and swollen from being caught in the giant's knee, and his right hand was burned shiny red through the tattered glove. "Oh, dear."

"The rest of me isn't much better," he said cheerfully.

"I haven't even ointment to put on the burns," Blanche sighed. She took a handkerchief from her cloak's pocket and dabbed at a welt on the side of his head. "Oh—that's nasty."

"It hurts." He twisted his head and grinned up at her.

"Oh, you're enjoying this," she groaned, blushing.

He gestured to hands and head, looking innocent. "What, this?"

She laughed, but a moment later she bent and kissed his forehead. "Thank you. Again."

Perceval cocked his head to look up at her, but then, on the wind, they heard the beat of galloping hooves. Instantly he struggled to his feet, gripping his sword. "Someone's coming."

The hooves rushed closer, as if blown on the wind. Through the shadowy orchard the fire's red glare struck glittering off mail. Then they saw the rider more clearly—a knight, sitting an outstretched white horse easily with slackened reins, his flashing sword whistling in the wind. Perceval snatched his own blade out of the sheath, but the knight had already reined in, throwing his horse into a sliding stop and coming to a dead halt within inches of Perceval's trembling swordpoint.

Spatters of mud settled back into the grass. With a titanic surge the horse regained its feet. The knight snatched off his helm and Blanche said in a voice that was half a sob:

"Sir Ector!"

Her guardian wiped his bloody sword against the saddle-blanket and shot it back into the sheath. "Blanche, my dear. Thank God we are not too late."

For the first time, Blanche saw two women who followed the knight and checked their horses more slowly. Nerys was one of them. The other, she guessed, must be the famous Nimue.

This was the one who spoke. "What happened here, sir?" she said, addressing Perceval.

"The servants think we are dead," he said. With the coming of their friends all the tight-wound vigilance had gone out of him, and his words slurred and stumbled against each other in weariness. "It was a giant. I don't know who sent him. He sleeps yonder," and he pointed to the flaming wreck of the house.

Sir Ector slid off Malaventure and gathered Blanche into his arm. "Well done," he said.

Perceval bowed his head. "What now? The servants have our horses. And I think you too have been hard-pressed."

Nimue said: "We were followed from Camelot, God knows how, for only the Council knew our errand. We went out of our way to shake them off, but Morgan and her men surprised us when I had opened the gate."

"Was there a fight?"

"For a while," rumbled Sir Ector, and Blanche shuddered at the fearful light in his eyes. "But her giant passed us easily enough."

"We put the others to flight and hastened through. The door is still open for us to return. As for the horses—" and Nimue put her hands to her mouth and sent a whisper into the wind. There was an answering whinny from the front lawn, a rush of hooves, and helpless gesticulations from the coachman's little black figure. A moment later, Rufus and Florence stood panting before them.

"Let us go," said Nimue.

In the sudden silence that followed the Lady's words Blanche glanced up to see that all of them had, almost involuntarily, turned to look at her. It took a moment for her to remember that she had once insisted on staying. A wry smile cracked the hot tight skin of her face.

"Yes, let's go," Blanche said.

S.D.G.

Blanche and Perceval will return in

The Quest for Carbonek

Now on sale!

The Great Houses of Britain

* - Knight of the Round Table

THE PENDRAGONS
  Uther Pendragon (deceased): The first High King of Britain.
  Igerne (deceased): Wife of (1) Gorlois, Duke of Tintagel, to whom she bore two daughters, Morgawse and Morgan, and (2) Uther Pendragon, to whom she bore a son, Arthur.
  * *Arthur Pendragon*: The High King of Britain, son of Uther Pendragon and Igerne.
  Guinevere: Daughter of King Leodigrance of Cameliard, wife of Arthur, mother of Blanchefleur.
  Blanchefleur: Daughter of Guinevere and, at least officially, the heir of Arthur Pendragon.

THE HOUSE OF ORKNEY
  King Lot of Orkney (deceased): The King of Orkney and husband of Morgawse.
  Morgawse: Half-sister of Arthur. Wife of Lot, to whom she bore four sons. Queen-regent of the isles of Orkney.
  * *Gawain*: The eldest son of Orkney, husband of Ragnell and father of Perceval.
  Ragnell: A fay of Avalon, wife of Gawain.
  * *Perceval*: Son of Gawain and Ragnell.
  * *Gaheris*: The second son of Orkney, husband of Lyonesse.

Lyonesse: Wife of Gaheris and sister of Lynet.

* *Gareth*: The third son of Orkney, husband of Lynet.

Lynet: Wife of Gareth and sister of Lyonesse.

* *Agravain*: The fourth son of Orkney.

THE HOUSE OF GORE

King Uriens of Gore: The King of Gore and husband of Morgan.

Morgan, commonly surnamed le Fay: Half-sister of Arthur. Estranged wife of Uriens, to whom she bore two sons. Queen of Gore.

* *Ywain*: The elder son of Gore.

* *Mordred*: The younger son of Gore.

THE HOUSE OF BRITTANY

King Ban of Brittany: Father of Bors and Ector de Maris. Uncle of Lancelot, Blamor, and Bleoberis.

* *Lancelot of the Lake*: Foster son of Nimue. Champion of Guinevere. Father of Galahad.

* *Galahad*: Son of Lancelot and Elaine of Carbonek.

* *Bors*: Cousin of Lancelot.

* *Lionel, Blamor, Bleoberis, Ector de Maris*: Cousins of Lancelot.

About the Author

Suzannah Rowntree lives in a big house in rural Australia with her awesome parents and siblings, reading academic histories of the Crusades and writing historical fantasy fiction that blends folklore and myth with historical fact.

You can connect with me on:
- https://suzannahrowntree.weebly.com
- https://twitter.com/suzannahtweets

Subscribe to my newsletter:
- https://www.subscribepage.com/srauthor

Made in the USA
Monee, IL
17 June 2021

71608218R00100